MW01114088

Curt Swarm

Task Force IED

Iowa National Guard's Fight Against IED's in Iraq

outskirts
press

Outskirts Press, Inc.
http://www.outskirtspress.com

Paperback ISBN: 978-1-9772-5554-9
Hardback ISBN: 978-1-9772-5555-6

Cover Image by Steve Helling

Outskirts Press and the "OP" logo are trademarks belonging to Outskirts Press, Inc.

Reviews

The exploits of the soldiers of the 451st Combat Engineering BN can be viewed as both funny and tragic. These accounts reflect the human challenges of deployed soldiers in believable detail. Curt Swarm does a masterful job in character development of a handful of soldiers assigned to the mythical 451 Combat Engineering BN deployed to Iraq. He illustrates how these characteristics reflect in different wartime experiences, both good and tragic. The accounts of unit personnel and their families upon their return to Iowa will make you both laugh and cry. The cost of war cannot be counted in just numbers, and this book illustrates war's human costs for the soldiers, their families, and their communities.

— Ken Madden, Colonel, US Army Retired

War is nothing new. War stories have been written for thousands of years, from the "Epic of Gilgamesh," "The Trojan War," "War and Peace" to "Guns for August." The common thread in any good book is the telling of a soldier's character; in the midst of war's profound physical and mental abuse that must be endured.

"Task Force IED" by Curt Swarm, takes on the challenge of telling his readers the complexities of a soldier's life; their initiation to the military interactions with fellow soldiers and officers, and their performance on the field of battle in Iraq.

But it is the story of the soldier's return home that is the real story of "Task Force IED." Captain Dingman, Sergeant Jones and Colonel

Price, are some of the characters whose destinies will forever be connected. They, the other members of the 451, and their families face a myriad of challenges back in Iowa. Substance abuse, alcoholism, divorce, depression, bankruptcy and suicide plagued some. Others prospered and were able to readjust to civilian life.

Curt Swarm develops his characters with language unique to each and paints a lasting image of their faith, politics, and true inner spirit. The human dimension spreads over the routine of the mission in Iraq to the aftermath of their deployment. Read Swarm's story and you understand why war changes not only the landscape but irrevocably changes people.

— Patty Madden, Retired School Teacher

"Task Force IED"--Historical Fiction based on a True Story — This story gripped me from the first paragraph until the last. This story shares the courage and resolve of the soldiers as they bravely face the daily challenges of "Task Force IED."

The reader is left with a sense of gratitude to those who serve in our military forces and the unbelievable circumstances they encounter and face every day. I found the story line riveting and characters compelling as they navigate the atrocities of war, a war with no way to gauge if you were winning. Does anyone really win a war?

Perhaps I am also left with the question, "Why do we choose to go to war?"

— Denise McCormick, 3 time number one best selling author of children's book, "Never Mind the Monkey Mind," Inspirational Speaker, and Educator's Coach.

Amazing. Shocking. Heartbreaking. This is a story seen through the eyes of men and women who came home from Iraq—changed permanently from who they were going into Iraq.

Curt Swarm holds nothing back in telling their stories as they were told to him by those "Warriors With Wings," and how they used their own PTSD to accomplish great things to help the returned warriors survive the aftermath of the hell of war—and the guilt of being a survivor.

Every citizen should read this book and then put their shoulders to the wheel in helping our returning soldiers heal from physical, emotional and mental injuries—starting with the VA!

—L. Kephart Nash, Retired RN,
Author of "When the Tempest Passes and the Wicked is No More"

Curt Swarm has written a gripping account of what some of the soldiers serving in Iraq experienced. He describes various events the soldiers dealt with while overseas, as well as issues these men and women faced as they tried to rejoin their lives once they came home. While this is a work of fiction, I know there is a strong basis of fact within these pages. Curt has captured the range of emotions these men and women have to endure every day. After reading his book I have a deeper understanding of what military service means.

—Susie Clark, Author of "And Then There Was One."

"Task Force IED" by Curt Swarm is a book that grabs your attention from the first chapter and does not let go until the end. It takes the reader on a roller coaster ride from the adrenaline highs of combat to the drug-filled lows of PTSD and veteran suicide. It covers the entire gamut of military experience in the Middle East, what some individual veterans encountered when they came back home, and it tells their story in a clear and sympathetic voice. As a military veteran and author, I highly recommend "Task Force IED."

—Gary B. Blackburn, Veteran
and Author of "Those Gentle Heroes"

Contents

Introduction

The war in the Middle East rapidly changed from a shooting conflict, and kicking in doors, to one of finding and destroying Improvised Explosive Devices (IED's). The IED's themselves rapidly changed from contact detonation devices (running over them with a vehicle or stepping on them) to ones that were triggered remotely, either through an electronic wire or hand held devices like cordless telephones.

I spent countless hours interviewing soldiers who served in the Middle East, ranging from Privates to Commanding Officers, both male and female. I have woven their stories into one, and used my imagination to fill in areas where I was lacking information. Any resemblance to actual people and events is purely coincidental. I was just needing to tell this story of the war against IED's, and the brave people who fought it.

Task Force IED is dedicated to all veterans, whether they served in war zones or not. As of this printing, 22 Middle East Veterans die by suicide everyday. Why this is happening is addressed in this story.

Please forgive me for using foul language. I tried to make this story as realistic as possible. People do talk this way in real life, especially soldiers in a far away land.

—Curt Swarm

16 Klicks

Captain Dingman looked at the data. It took him a while to realize what he was looking at. What appeared to be random IED (Improvised Explosive Device) detonations and occasional sniper attacks across the country of Iraq, with U.S. soldiers being killed, injured and maimed, were in actuality, very predictable Significant Events (SE's). He played with the software some more, and fiddled with an algorithm, writing a new one. In essence, he was asking, through an algorithm, "From point A to point B, where will be the IED's on such-and-such a date and such-and-such a time?" Bingo. A shiver ran up his spine, and the back of his neck tingled. In plain, graphic detail, there was the answer.

Dingman took it a step further. "On such-and-such a date, from point A to point B, where will be the fewest IED's?" Bingo again. He felt his rectum tighten. How could this be? It was so simple. The entire Army had been working on problems such as this, with this same data base, and never came up with anything close to what he was looking at.

Captain Dingman, the 451's S-2 Intel officer, picked up the phone to call Sergeant Jones, his right-hand man in Intel. Then he stopped. "Better sleep on it," he told himself. "This is too simple. There's got to be something wrong. The whole fricking War Department can't come up with this, but I can—a little ole National Guard soldier from Iowa? Hmm. I'll sleep on it."

Dingman laid down on the bunk he had in his work area and tried to sleep. It was 3:00 am (0300 in military time). He kept seeing data numbers and different colored push pins, Significant

Events. After 15 minutes of numbers running through his head, he sat up, grabbed the phone and dialed Sergeant Jones.

"Jonesie? Get your ass over here. I got something to show you."

Sergeant Jones hadn't been able to sleep either. He had been watching Blue Force Tracker. His step son was on a night mission south of Ramadi. Even though Junior was his wife's son, Jonesie loved him like his own son that he never had. In fact, Jonesie had been instrumental in getting Junior into the Guard, something that was a sticky point with Jonesie's wife. Junior was with a convoy escort using the Buffalo to clear IED's. One misstep and it would be Foo Bar, something Jonesie's wife would never forgive him for.

"What the fuck?" Jonesie mumbled in the phone. He tried to make his voice sound like he had been asleep. "It's oh 300."

Dingman said, "You gotta see this."

They both looked at the data. Sergeant Jones finally spoke. "You mean to fucking-A tell me, sir, that you took off-the-shelf software, wrote a fricking algorithm, plugged it into the biggest God damned data base the military has, and you can predict where the IED's are, anywhere in Iraq?"

"It appears so, Jonesie."

"Quick. Run these coordinates. Junior is out there right now."

Captain Dingman punched the numbers in.

Sergeant Jones' lower jaw dropped. "Get Ops to abort that mission now, sir. Junior's running into a trap. Abort now!"

Captain Dingman did as his sergeant asked (or told him). Dingman had complete trust in anything his NCO did or wanted. "Price is going to want an explanation. We better have our assholes wired tight."

At 0600 Colonel Price had Captain Dingman and Sergeant Jones at attention. "You stopped that convoy because you," (he pointed a finger at Captain Dingman) "took the entire data base of all the SE's in the entire fucking country of Iraq, something the whole frigging war department, with all its manpower and computers and programmers hasn't been able to do, and you can predict where IED's are located?"

"I think so, sir," was all Captain Dingman could say.

"You think? You stopped a convoy in the middle of the night because you think?"

Colonel Price was teetering on the verge of ordering Captain Dingman and Sergeant Jones to shut down what he considered to be a quack project they had no business or authority monkeying with, or to let them go ahead with what might be the game changer in the war in Iraq. Colonel Price knew, of course, what Captain Dingman's background was in the civilian world. Dingman was a Six Sigma Black Belt, a top notch statistical-computer-analysis-number-crunching-guru sumbitch. "Just where the hell and how did you get this top secret data base?"

Price looked first at Captain Dingman, who had a blank look on his face and was starting to go pale, then at Sergeant Jones. Sergeant Jones was sweating. "Jonesie, did you...?"

"I acquired it, sir."

"Acquired it? You mean you stole it—a top secret data base of all the Significant Events in the whole freaking country of Iraq, of all the IED explosions, all the sniper killings, all the gun shots, all the suicides, and you can tell me what's going to happen on a twenty mile stretch of desert between Ramadi and Timbuktu?"

"Within 80 percent accuracy, sir," Captain Dingman shot out.

"80 percent, huh? Well, your 80 percent might get you a court martial. Do you understand? Get that Buffalo going and see what's out there ahead of that convoy that you were so sure was headed into a trap. And you Fucking-A better be right or your ass is grass and I'll be the lawn mower. Do you understand, Captain Dingman and Sergeant Jones?"

"Yes, sir."

"Yes, sir."

As it turned out, the buffalo, a giant mobile machine for finding, removing and detonating IED's, found a hornets' nest of IED's ahead of that convoy. Sergeant Jones brought out his favorite Montague cigars and gave one to Captain Dingman.

As they were lighting up, Colonel Price walked in. Dingman and Jones snapped to attention, cigars still in their mouths.

Colonel Price looked at them and fought back a grin. The cigar smoke smelled good, great actually. He was terribly home sick. "You got one of them for me, or are you just sucking dick?"

"Yes, sir, sir."

Both Dingman and Jones offered to light the Colonel's cigar.

Even though he knew he wasn't supposed to, Colonel Price inhaled the cigar smoke deeply. It felt good and made him dizzy. He blew a smoke ring, and then another. Uncannily, the smoke rings linked.

Dingman and Jones observed this special smoking trick of their Colonel's and knew he was in deep thought.

Colonel Price spoke up. "Get Lieutenant Dobbs in here. He's got a convoy going out tonight. He may want to see this."

Lieutenant Dobbs was a brilliant officer who was bucking for Captain. At five-foot eight, he was rather short and a little pudgy, but could be mean as a snake or as sweet as honey, depending on the situation. His platoon knew this and adored him. And Dobbs was fiercely protective of his men.

He studied the data Dingman and Jones gave him. "You mean to tell me," Dobbs was incredulous, "that the IED's are here, here and here?" He pointed at different points on the route his convoy was going to take that night. "I am to stop here and here, and advance at this time? And this set of IED's is pressure activated and these are remote?"

"We think so, Lieutenant," Captain Dingman said. "Give it a try. Better'n running blind, ain't it?"

"How do you know this, Dingman?" Lieutenant Dobbs asked.

"It's patterns," Captain Dingman told him. "SE's are not random at all, like most people think. If you analyze them statistically, you can see patterns and repeats, to a point. It's not a hundred percent, but it beats the shit out of having nothing at all. Wouldn't you agree, Dobbs? Give it a try."

Lieutenant Dobbs did. His convoy got through their mission without a hiccup and they found and removed three IED's, IED's that could have killed and maimed a number of U.S. soldiers. Lieutenant Dobbs was convinced.

Colonel Price told Captain Dingman and Sergeant Jones to prepare a Power-Point presentation and get it up to Duckworth, the Marine General in charge of military ops in Iraq. Price would approve it. And he told them, "You'd better have all your t's crossed and your i's dotted."

Sergeant Jones was Captain Dingman's Intel Sergeant and right hand man. Jones, or Jonesie as he was called, was a natural when it came to computers and thinking logically. He had no formal training with computers, mathematics or statistics but he thought like a computer, operated like one, and could be as unemotional as one (on the surface). When it came to writing the algorithms and scrubbing data that came to them daily, Sergeant Jones was like a machine. He could visualize the landscape that the data was portraying, almost like a third eye.

In actuality, Captain Dingman was Sergeant Jones' right hand man. Dingman was the officer, of course, and Jones the NCO, but Sergeant Jones had been responsible for whipping Captain Dingman into shape and making him into a first rate officer. When Dingman first came to him as a First Lieutenant, Jones was hell on him. Dingman couldn't do anything right, but they were forming a relationship that would be so successful that they actually turned the fight in Iraq, which was a war against IED's, to the United States' favor—these two Iowa National Guard soldiers—"Weekend Warriors" they were called by the regular Army.

But the National Guard brought to the table something the regular Army had little of, and that was the practical experience they had gained in the civilian world. Regular Army soldiers, as a rule, typically had very little real life experience, having enlisted right out of high school or college. Dingman brought with him his Six Sigma Black Belt experience in statistical analysis and Jones his experience as a survivor and a street fighter. The regular Army soldiers were good at PT (Physical Training), but that was about it, as far as Jones was concerned, who struggled to keep his weight down.

Captain Dingman and Sergeant Jones worked night and day for three days preparing a power-point presentation. It was 131 pages long and took up 3.1 gigs of computer space. You better believe they had every "t" crossed and every "i" dotted. It was a beautiful Power Point presentation, laying out in precise, logical detail the how and why statistical analysis of every Significant

Event in Iraq. It highlighted patterns and relationships that could be used in predicting, within 80% accuracy, where and when future IED's would go off.

Both Dingman and Jones were scared as hell. They knew they were breaking every chain-of-command regulation by sending their power point directly to General Duckworth, even with Colonel Price's approval. By military regs it should go up one level, be approved, then up to the next level, be approved, and so on. But this was a life-or-death situation. U.S. Soldiers were fighting, dying and being maimed every day at the hands of bomb making insurgents. The faster Dingman and Jones could get their program into the hands of someone who had the authority to do something about it, countrywide, the more lives could be saved.

Actually it was Dingman who was scared. He had his mind set on a military career that would take him to the top and he didn't want anything to derail it. But then again, this discovery of his and Jones could propel him even faster.

Jones, the street fighter, on the other hand, was for all-balls-out tactics and to let the chips fall where they may. In street fighting, there are no rules, and the faster you can over power your opponent, no matter what dirty tricks you have to use, the more likely you are to come out on top. This philosophy had served him well as a river rat growing up, all through boot camp and Advanced Infantry Training (AIT), and progressing through the ranks. If nothing else, he gained the respect of his opponent or enemy — they knew they'd have their hands full if they took him on — and that he wouldn't back down or give up no matter what.

They sent the power-point package to Colonel Price. Price barely glanced through it. He already knew enough of Dingman and Jones that they would do a stellar job of presenting their case in graphic detail. As he was glancing through the Power-Point presentation, a vision popped into his head. It was of his cigar smoke forming two linked circles. In the vision a third circle of smoke appeared and looped with the other two, forming three circles—an extremely rare feat. Price had only seen this done once, by a professional cigar smoker who was bet $1,000 he couldn't do it.

Colonel Price hit the send button.

Marine General Duckworth saw the 3.1 gig file in his in-folder. He knew it would take a half hour to download, maybe longer. What the hell was anybody doing sending him a file this large? He didn't have time to mess with it. He deleted it.

It wasn't until he was lying in bed, unable to sleep that he couldn't get the 3.1 gig file out of his head. If someone had balls enough to send him a file that large, it must be worth looking at. Maybe it was porn. He got out of bed and found the deleted file in his trash folder. He opened it, and then went back to bed while it was down loading.

In the morning he took a look at it. He couldn't believe what he was seeing. Who in the hell were Captain Dingman and Sergeant Jones? The coding indicated they were Iowa National Guard soldiers. What business did they have sending him anything?

However, he had to admit, that what he was looking at piqued his interest. Something about statistical analysis of SE's used to predict future SE's. Hmm. Maybe he'd better make a trip to Ramadi and see just who in the hell this Dingman and Jones were. He knew Colonel Price, barely. But Dingman and Jones?

He picked up the phone. "Morgan?" he said to his Colonel. "Get the chopper ready. We're going to Ramadi."

Duckworth and his entourage stepped off the chopper. "I

want to see this Dingman and Jones," he told Colonel Price, who was there to meet him.

Price had Dingman and Jones front and center real fast. They stood at attention as Duckworth dressed them down. "Just what in the hell do you mean sending me this 3.1 gig file that took half-an-hour to download that doesn't even have any skin in it? Don't you know I have better things to do? There's a fucking war going on here, and I don't have time to be piddly fucking around with no Iowa National Guard."

"Yes, sir, sir."

"You've got 15 minutes of my time, and you'd better make good use of it or I know a couple of grunts who are going to be peeling potatoes."

"Yes, sir, sir."

With that, Dingman jumped in with both feet. He had Jones running the Power Point as he explained why and how Significant Events, that appeared to be random, were actually very predictable events that had patterns, patterns that could be used to locate and disarm IED's. Dingman made sure he included Jones. If Dingman was going to go down, he would take Jones with him.

"Sixteen klicks," Dingman told General Duckworth. "If you can control what goes on in sixteen-by-sixteen kilometers, you can control the whole Goddamned country."

General Duckworth listened with what appeared to be bored attention, his arms crossed over his belly.

Dingman actually took 17 minutes to get through the 131 Power-Point pages. When he was done, as is customary, he asked the General, "Do you have any questions, sir?"

Duckworth looked at his watch and noted that Dingman had gone past the 15 minutes.

Both Dingman and Jones thought they were dead meat.

However, Duckworth turned to his Colonel and asked, "Colonel Morgan, how many men do you have working for you?"

Colonel Morgan stammered, "Well, er, ah, sir, I have 32 men and women working for me, sir."

"32 men and women." General Duckworth seemed to be digesting this number. "You mean to tell me these two soldiers from the Iowa National Guard can do something your whole department, with all their computers, and programmers, can't? They can take off-the-fucking-shelf software, plug it into our data base, and can tell me when and where the next IED's are going to go off?"

"I'll have to study the data some more, sir," Morgan sputtered.

"Study the data? You've studied it enough. I want Dingman and Jones in front of your department today showing them how in the hell to do their job. Do you understand me, Colonel Morgan?"

"Yes, sir, sir."

With that, the fight against IED's and the war in Iraq turned.

Dingman and Jones and their handful of intelligence soldiers became real popular real fast, not only in Ramadi, the most dangerous hell hole in Iraq and the world, but throughout the whole country of Iraq. For every convoy that went out, every mission that was started, especially IED finding missions, the platoon leader would send a message or be at the door of Jones' intelligence shack wanting maps of where IED's were, what kind they were, and what to expect.

Sergeant Jones would input the information in algorithm form of where and when they were going, and then print out huge topographical maps (on a stolen printer) of every hiccup and fart they could expect along the way.

Captain Dingman was sent all over Iraq to give instructions on how to use the data, and how to create it. He was lovingly, or not so lovingly, called "Captain Dingy."

All-in-all, the 451st National Guard Engineering Battalion from NE Iowa was credited with finding and disarming 831 IED's, a phenomenal number and accomplishment, something for which Dingman and Jones would receive Bronze Stars. Countless lives were saved and injuries prevented.

Dingman summoned Sergeant Jones into his office. "Jonesie, there are going to be some men coming in to see you. They probably won't look like soldiers, but they are. They're Seals. Just give them what they want."

"Yes, sir."

Sergeant Jones couldn't believe what was standing in front of him. The man, if you could call him a man, was dressed like an Iraqi Insurgent, with full beard, head covering and sandals. He smelled so bad it burned Jones' nostrils. It smelled like salt. The soldier was also carrying an M-16 with his finger in the trigger guard. Jones noticed that the safety was off. "Er, ah," Jones stammered. "Could you put the safety on?"

"My finger is the safety," the man grunted.

Jones thought, "So this is a Seal?"

It came out that the Seal wanted specific information on a certain bomb maker: who he was, and where he could be found, at what hours.

Jones ran the algorithm and gave it to him.

The Seal turned and left without saying thank you.

Jones said, "Go get'm, Tiger," to his back.

But Dingman and Jones needed more data on IED's. They had Lieutenant Dobbs in the office with them, along with Colonel Price. Jones gave Dobbs the news he didn't want to hear. "Instead of keeping moving, if an IED goes off, we want you to stop and investigate the scene. Record and take pictures of anything you see. What kind of wire was used, how many turns it has, were there solder connections? We think if we can get more data on IED's we can refine our accuracy even more, say from 80% to 85, even 90%."

"You want me to stop?" Dobbs couldn't believe what he was hearing. "And investigate? We'll be sitting ducks. Snipers will have a field day. The way to save lives, Captain Dingman, er, ah, no disrespect, sir, is to keep moving."

"I know. I know," Captain Dingman sighed. "We want you to be crime-scene investigators, like on CSI. Get us more data and we think we can save even more lives."

Colonel Price was nodding his head in agreement.

Dobbs shook his head. Stopping a moving convoy after an explosion violated every rule of warfare and survival he had been taught. He didn't say it, but he thought it, "These computer nerds are carrying their pet statistics way too far. Dingman is dingy."

"It's an order, Lieutenant Dobbs," Colonel Price told him.

Lieutenant Dobbs saluted, did an about face, and left without saying another word.

They were two hours into their mission when an IED went off between them and the next vehicle up front, causing little damage. There was always a 50 meter distance maintained between vehicles so that an IED wouldn't damage more than one vehicle. It was obvious that the insurgent sitting out there somewhere with his cordless phone had mistimed his detonation. Lucky for Dobbs and his men.

They did what they were told and stopped to collect data on the SE. They were taking pictures and recording the depth and diameter of the blast hole, and other miscellaneous information.

One of the soldiers with them was from another platoon, a Marine Lieutenant, John Washington, an Afro American. He was just along for the ride. He was going home on leave and was catching a ride with Dobbs' convoy to the air strip. Washington was good natured and easy going. He jumped in and helped Dobbs and his men collect data, although he didn't have to.

It was Lieutenant Washington who found the wire. It was buried in the sand and barely sticking up like a baby garter snake. "Whata we got here?" he said out loud. "Lookie here, Dobbs."

Lieutenant Dobbs looked at the wire and began pulling it up. It meandered off into the desert. He looked at Washington, and Washington looked back, cocking his eyebrows up and down.

Washington said, "Are you thinking what I'm thinking?"

"I think so," Dobbs was blunt. "If we fucking-A follow this wire, we might just find us a bomb making mother-fucker."

"That's what I'm thinking, too," said Washington, who had no business helping this platoon. He was on his way home to visit his wife and kids. He had a new baby boy he had never seen.

They began pulling the wire up and advancing into the desert, followed by two soldiers in a Humvee. They had gone about 400 meters when the blast blew the Humvee over, killing Lieutenant John Washington, also Herman Stein a Spec 5, and seriously wounding a medic who was accompanying the convoy. Dobbs was knocked off his feet, but was mostly unhurt except for his uniform smoking, and he couldn't hear for awhile.

It was a trap and they had walked right into it.

Dobbs caught Sergeant Jones in the intelligence shack the next morning. Dobbs was still wearing his tattered camo fatigues with burn holes, and there was dried blood around his nostrils and one ear hole. "You did this," he told Jones. "If it weren't for you and your fucking data collection, these men would still be alive. I hope you're happy."

Jones didn't know what to say. Dobbs was right. These men would still be alive if it weren't for him and Dingman. Of course, he didn't tell them to follow that wire, and it was Colonel Price who had given the order to stop and investigate, but Jones kept his mouth shut. Dobbs was in no mood for rationale or logic. Sergeant Jones felt like he had blood on his hands.

Dobbs turned and walked away. From then on, there was a faraway look in Dobbs' eye. He went about his duties, but talked little. There was something missing. And he never, ever came back to Jones and Dingman again for information on where IED's were located.

Jones had nightmares and couldn't sleep, but kept it to himself. Soldiers didn't talk about their feelings.

Colonel Price, knowing the cost of war, told Dingman and Jones to keep doing what they were doing, that they had saved more lives by far than had been taken.

"Let's call this Task Force IED," he told them.

Good-Time Charlie

"We gotta get that sumbitch," Captain Kurt Dingman told Sergeant Dwight Jones.

Dwight shook his head in agreement.

They were both in shock and hurting real bad. Two men were dead, one of them the 451's, the other a Marine on his way home and just needing a ride to the airstrip. A couple of other soldiers were injured so bad it wasn't known if they would live or not. The worst part was they were following a route Dwight had told them was safe. It led right into a trap.

Dwight had never known such feelings of hurt, grief, shame, guilt, responsibility, you-name-it, all rolled into one black nightmare. He wanted to die. Everybody knew their Intel was 80% accurate. That 20% had just gotten real.

Dingman put his hand on Dwight's shoulder. "What intel you got on that motherfucker?"

"Not much. Up until now he's caused little damage—a blown tire here, a dud explosion there, maybe a rollover—a real Good-Time Charlie. He doesn't seem to know what he's doing. His IED's are faulty and poorly built, not to mention ill-placed. He either got lucky on this one, or he's smarter than we think, or he's get'n smarter."

"Give me something to go on." Dingman was serious. "A vehicle, where he might live, is he a loner or does he work with others? Anything."

"We think he's on a motorcycle."

"A motorcycle?"

"Yeah. From the air-reconnaissance I'm seeing a single tire track in the sand. It's gotta be a murdercycle."

"You sure?"

Dwight stared at the floor. "I was sure the route Stein and Washington were taking was safe. Look where it got..."

"Don't be so hard on yourself, Dee," (Dee was one of Dwight's nicknames). Dingman put his hand on Dwight's shoulder again. This was as close to a hug as they would allow themselves. Men didn't hug. "This is war. It ain't purdy. People get killed and injured. We do the best we can with what we have. We make the best decision we can at the time. It usually works, sometimes it don't. You've saved a lot of lives. The odds were bound to catch up with us. Get'n that sumbitch won't bring Stein and Washington back, but it sure as hell will make us feel better."

"What you gonna do?" asked Dwight.

"He set a trap. I'm gonna set a trap. See if I can catch Good-Time Charlie."

"Yeah?"

"I'm go'n out there in the desert with Fonze and Clinton. Lay in the desert for a day or two, maybe three. See what pokes its head up."

"Can I go with you? I wanna pull the trigger."

"Naw, Dee. You gotta keep give'n safe routes to convoys. I need you here running Task Force IED."

"Well, here then." Dwight grabbed his spare clip. "Use my ammo. Get that bastard with my bullet."

"You got it, Dee."

Captain Dingman spent a day rounding up Fonze and Clinton and getting ready—chopper insertion, night vision, camo, pick-up date, location. Each soldier was to carry his own supplies.

Clinton was one tough son-of-a-bitch, a real Captain America. Dingman saw him do a hundred push-ups one day, the last 25 with hand-claps, without hardly breaking a sweat. That was impressive.

Dingman noticed Captain America wasn't carrying much water.

"Where's your water?" he asked.

Clinton gave a little laugh, "Aw, I'm gonna see if I can get by on 12 ounces a day. I think I can do it."

"Twelve ounces? Are you crazy? It's 115, 120 degrees out there."

"Yeah, I know. I like to travel light."

Dingman shook his head. Clinton liked to push the limits, live on the edge. Dingman hoped he knew what he was doing, that he didn't push it too far. Out there on the desert, not only could it cost Clinton his life, but the lives of others, namely himself and Fonzy.

They got inserted into the middle of nowhere, and picked a high spot where they could dig in and survey a couple of convoy routes. They would spell each other. Then it was a matter of watching and waiting.

The heat was murder, and under camo tarps it was even worse. Dingman felt like they were cooking. They actually were.

"Where you from?" Dingman asked Clinton.

"Cedar Rapids."

"You play high school sports?"

"Oh, yeah. Football, baseball, track."

"Track? You ran track, as big as you are?"

"Shot put and discus. I hate running."

"You got a scholarship, too. Didn't you?"

"Yeah, Iowa State. I was gonna be a first ever three-sport college athlete—catcher in baseball—my batting average was .411, tight end in football—13 touchdowns, and shot put in track—state record. They were gonna let me flip-flop baseball and track practice. One night baseball, the next night track. Track meets and ball games would be tricky, but they were gonna try. Some meets and games I would miss, but they would work around it. Studying didn't matter. I was gonna be Iowa State's three-sport poster boy."

"No shit. What happened?"

"Blew out an ACL, last game for Cedar Rapids-Jefferson. Major reconstruction. It was over."

"Aw, that's too bad."

Clinton shrugged his shoulders. "No biggie. My parents wanted me to be a lawyer anyway."

"A lawyer?" This surprised Dingman. Clinton didn't seem to have the smarts for a lawyer.

"Yeah, so I went to the University of Iowa, fell in love with a cheerleader and she dumped me. It hurt worse than the ACL. I dropped out of college middle of second semester. My grades were shit anyway. I couldn't concentrate. All I could think about was how I was gonna kill the asshole she dumped me for—a premed student—strangle him with my bare hands or hang'm up by the balls. It was really screwing with my head."

"Jesus Christ."

"Got a job with Deere, like my dad. He got me the job actually, and joined the Guard, also like my dad. So here I am cooking my ass."

"What about you, Fonze?" Dingman asked. "What's your story?"

His real name was Foster, but everyone called him Fonze or Fonzy, like the television character, Henry Winkler, because he was a pretty boy and was always looking at himself in the mirror—combing his hair, what little there was. The Guard didn't allow long hair or sideburns.

"Me? Factory worker by day, motor cycle gang at night. We had a bike club. I ain't shitting you when I say I was the leader of the motorcycle gang, Iowa Hogs. I was the guy the others asked, 'What we doing tonight? Where we going?' We all rode Harley-Hogs, some chopped. We would terrorize places like the truck stop at Walcott—world's largest, they say—get in fights with truckers, crash parties, bar fights, get the cops after us. The judge told me, 'Military or Jail. Your choice.' So, here I am. Hot, ain't it?"

Dingman shook his head. He always marveled at the different backgrounds of men, or men and women, in the Guard.

Fonze and Clinton looked at Dingman. "So what's your story, Captain?"

"Me? Not much. I was gonna be a construction worker, build houses, shit like that, until I saw what it could do to my body. My dad, or my real dad—my mom and dad were divorced—was a college professor. He got me into college, tuition free. The college had a perk—employees' kids went free, no matter their high school grades. It was a black college, and ROTC was mandatory. I could be an 'ocifer.' So I thought, 'What the fuck?' Here I am. Oh, one more thing."

"What's that?" Fonze asked.

Dingman took off his helmet, leaned forward, and ran his finger across his eyebrows. Sweat poured off in a stream. It was a farmer move he had learned baling hay as a kid. He ran his hand across the top of his sweaty head and wiped his hand on his blouse. "I always got D's and F's in math in high school. My dad was a math professor in college. I was sorta an embarrassment to him. In college, I had to take remedial math. I got an A. I went on to get straight A's in math, and my degree is in math. Go figure. All that math and statistics is what led Jones and me to develop our computer analysis of IED locations, Task Force

IED. When you can apply something abstract to a practical application, it makes more sense. Except it got a couple of guys killed, which is why we're here."

Clinton spoke up. "The Twin Towers is why we're here, Cap'n."

"You got that right," Fonze added. "We trained them camel jocks to fly our airplanes so they could fly'm into our towers. Wham-bam, thank-you, ma'am."

They sat silent for awhile, thinking.

There was the whop-whop sound of chopper blades behind them. They turned around. A cobra was hovering, training on them.

"Jesus Christ!" Fonze screamed. "Where's the fucking strobe? The strobe!"

Dingman dug frantically in his pack, tearing at it like a wild animal.

Clinton was waving his arms. "Don't shoot, motherfucker! It's us!"

Dingman came up with the strobe and flipped the switch for infra-red.

The cobra dipped its rotors, like saying, "Okie dokie, guys, just checking," and was gone, as fast as it appeared.

"Fuck-a-duck!" screamed Fonze. "We could'a been toast!"

"Yeah, but it would've been quick," Dingman philosophized. "Painless."

They all thought about it for a moment.

Dingman spoke first, "I don't know what happened. They were supposed to know we were here. Something got fucked-up somewhere."

"Oh, man," Clinton sighed. "I near shit my pants."

"Why is it?" Fonze wanted to know. "The good guys clobber themselves as much as the enemy does?"

Dingman whispered, "I have seen the enemy and he is me."

Fonze and Clinton, looked at each other, and shrugged their shoulders.

Clinton had his binoculars trained on the horizon. "Something's moving, three o'clock."

They all trained their binoculars in that direction.

"Looks like an ant, skittering around," Fonze said.

As they watched, the figure grew larger until they could tell it was someone on a motorcycle.

"Looks like a 125 Suck Zuki," Fonze spat. "Wish I had my boys here, the Hogs. We'd lasso, what did you call him? Good-Time-Charlie? And drag his ass until he was dead."

The figure stopped. Good-Time-Charlie got off his motorcycle, walked to a spot, and it looked like he was burying something.

"That's him. Motherfucker," Fonze hissed. "Let's get'm, Cap'n."

"No wait," Dingman told him. "Let's see what he does."

The figure threw some camo over his bike and melted into the sand.

"That's him!" Fonze screamed. "That's him, Cap'n!"

Dingman hushed him. Even though they were over a mile away, Dingman was afraid Good-Time-Charlie could hear them. "Be quiet, Fonze. Sound travels on the desert."

"Oh, right, Cap'n. Sorry. Call in the Cobra and fry his ass."

Dingman thought about it. It would be easy. Poof. Gone. "Naw, I wanna look this motherfucker in the eye. Let the cock-sucker know who got'm and why. Ready for action, boys?"

"Fuck'n-A," hissed Fonze.

There was no sound from Clinton.

Dingman looked at him. Clinton had stopped sweating and was white as a sheet.

Dingman knew the signs of heat exhaustion from when he worked construction. "Drink some water, Clinton. You look like shit."

Clinton held up his one bottle. It was empty.

"God damn you, Clinton. A man your size needs plenty of water. Why didn't you bring more?"

Clinton shrugged his big shoulders. "I think I fucked up."

"Ya think? Here, drink some of mine," and handed his bottle to Clinton.

Clinton put it to his lips, took a swig and spit it out. "Too hot," he said. "I'm gonna be sick." He leaned forward and puked up stinky green stuff.

"Jesus Christ, Clinton," Dingman barked. "You're gonna ruin this mission. It's a day-and-a-half before pick up."

"Sorry, Cap'n," Clinton whispered. "You guys go ahead. I'll stay here."

Dingman thought about what to do. It would be real simple to call in an air strike on Good-Time Charlie. It would be all over, quick. And Dingman could call in an early pick-up and get Clinton the hell out. But Dingman wanted Good-Time Charlie in his sights real bad, with Jonesie's ammo.

Dingman and Fonze belly crawled toward the figure, hiding behind high spots in the desert for cover. They were pretty sure Good-Time-Charlie had his eyes trained on the convoy route, so they approached in opposite directions, Dingman from the side, Fonze from the rear.

When they got closer, Dingman trained his binoculars on Good-Time-Charlie. He looked skinny, underfed, with a scruffy beard. He was holding a cordless phone in his hand. In Iraq, cordless phones had a far greater range than in the

United States—up to half-a-mile, sometimes further, if they were "souped up."

Dingman crawled real slow, not wanting to be seen. He hoped Fonze was doing the same. When Dingman got within 100 meters, he stood up with his rifle to his shoulder, and the cross hairs trained on Good-Time-Charlie. It appeared like Good-Time-Charlie might be asleep, or praying. His eyes were closed and he was sitting cross-legged with his hands on his knees, palms up. The cordless phone was in his left hand.

Dingman got within 25 meters of Good-Time-Charlie's left side. Dingman could hear him now. He was chanting. Dingman purposely coughed. Good-Time-Charlie shot up and turned in the opposite direction of Dingman. When Good-Time-Charlie didn't see anything, Dingman coughed again. This time Good-Time-Charlie spun around and faced Dingman. When he saw Dingman had a rifle trained on him, he held up his hands. "Pleeds," he mumbled in broken English "My fambly."

Dingman plugged him right in the chest.

"Washington and Stein had 'famblies' too, you son-of-a-bitch," Dingman hissed.

Fonzy jumped up out of nowhere. "You got'm, Cap'n," he screeched. "You got'm!"

They both approached real slow, their rifles trained on the body, which was twitching. The cordless phone had flown out of his hand, so they knew he couldn't detonate the IED.

"Jesus Christ!" Fonzy croaked. "He didn't even have a gun. He's out here with just a fucking bomb and chickenshit bike."

"It appears that way," Dingman said.

Good-Time-Charlie was still moving a little. His eyes were open. He was trying to reach into one of his pockets.

"Don't move, cocksucker!" Fonzy yelled. "We'll blow your shit away!"

Good-Time-Charlie's fingers reached his pocket and held something. Dingman and Fonzy could tell it wasn't a gun. It was a little black Koran.

"Well, I'll be Goddamned," Dingman said.

Good-Time-Charlie was holding it toward them. He mumbled, "Geeve to my fambly."

Good-Time-Charlie expired. His blood soaking into the desert as fast as it was pumping out.

Dingman and Fonzy both stared. They didn't know what to say. Both were so numb their feelings were blocked.

They spent the rest of the day digging out the IED. There was no worry about it going off with the cordless phone in their possession.

A convoy of Marines came by. Dingman radioed them, identified himself, and had them stop. Dingman showed them the IED they could have run into and Good-Time-Charlie's body.

"Let me show you how this little jewel works." he told them. The IED was about 25 meters away on the surface of the desert. Dingman triggered the cordless phone. The concussion from the blast nearly knocked all of them over and showered them with sand and dust.

"Jesus Christ!" the Lieutenant of the Marines coughed. "You're the Iowa National Guard, you killed an insurgent, and detonated his IED that was waiting for us?"

"Yep'r," Dingman said. "But I want to tell you something. It doesn't feel as good as I thought it would."

"What do you mean?"

"I'm not sure he's any different than any one of us. Just a poor shit out here trying to earn a buck to feed his 'fambly.'"

They were all silent, letting the words soak in.

Dingman left Good-Time-Charlie's body with the Marines. He heard later they took credit for the kill.

It didn't matter. Dingman had more important things on his mind. He had Clinton to deal with, who had gone from Heat Exhaustion to Heat Stroke. By the time Dingman got the Blackhawk called in to pick them up, Clinton was delirious. But he lived — not much wiser for his near-death experience. He continued to push the limits and eventually got killed in a whorehouse in New York, which didn't surprise Dingman.

Back at camp, Dwight was waiting for them. "Heard you got'm with my bullet," Dwight chortled. "Good-Fuck'n-Time Charlie. Good work. Wish I'd been there."

Dingman didn't respond. And from the look on Dingman's face, and his silence, Dwight knew not to push it.

Dingman, the statistician, whispered, "They kill us, we kill them. What's the difference? Net zero."

Six Sigma Black Belt

He grew up in Alabama, Kurt Dingman. His parents divorced at an early age, and his mother, whom he lived with, remarried. His step father, as well as his father, were both good men and treated him well.

Growing up in Alabama, many of his friends were black. When Kurt looked at a person, he didn't see black or white, he saw a person. He and his friends fished and played sandlot everything. It was an idyllic childhood, really. There were lemonade stands, fist fights and experimental sex.

Kurt was never a good student, terrible actually. He did only enough to get by and never, ever took homework home. D's were his highest grade, which didn't bother him. In fact, he and his friends, most of them black, sort of made fun of the "egg heads."

Spurning college prep classes, Kurt took Industrial Arts or Shop. As a junior and senior, his class built a home and sold it, which was good experience. As a senior, he spent half the day working for a contractor. Kurt liked to make money.

It was while working for this contractor, which he enjoyed for the most part, that he began to wake up to what his future might be. It happened when they were pouring a double-wide concrete driveway. It was stinking hot—over a 100 degrees in the shade, actual. Sweat was pouring off Kurt in rivulets, stinging his eyes, and blurring his work, which was hand troweling concrete. Kurt didn't need to add any water to the too-fast drying concrete because his sweat was supplying that.

Then he wasn't sweating, and he felt strangely good, happy even, and a little light headed. He noticed he felt cold, and had goose bumps, which was strange in the heat. A sickness sort of went through him like he might throw up. He started to stand up, and his legs buckled. That's the last thing he remembered.

He came to under a shade tree with Roscoe, the man he was working with, looking down on him.

"What happened?" Kurt asked.

"Too much heat," Roscoe laughed. "You weren't drinking 'nuff and you need a hat. Here, drink some of dis." Roscoe handed him a cup of water from the cooler. Kurt drank some, then poured the rest over his head and down the back of his neck, sending shock waves through his hot body.

"Dat's good, dat's good," Roscoe told him. "Here, take 'nother."

Kurt noticed how big and gnarly Roscoe's hands were — the cup appearing tiny in them, his knuckles almost as big as the cup. In his other hand, Roscoe had a Marlboro Red. He chain smoked, lighting one off the other during his break of looking after "the white boy."

"Lemmie ask you something, Roscoe," Kurt asked.

"What's dat?"

"What'r you going to do tonight when you get off work?"

"What am I going to do? Ha! I'm going to pop me a quart of Truckweiser, drink it, then have 'nother, and probably 'nother, before I pass out. Why?"

"Just wondering. What about tomorrow night?"

"Same ting. And the night after dat, and the night after dat."

"Huh," Kurt thought. "Day after day."

Kurt's dad, his real dad, was a math professor at Tuskegee University, a mostly black university in Tuskegee, Alabama. He called Kurt and said, "Tomorrow's the last day you can register here. You get a free ride 'cause you're my kid. What else you gonna do? Give it a try."

"College?" Kurt was about to say he would rather build houses, but a little sick feeling went through him, like the feeling he had just before he fainted from the heat. He thought about Roscoe, going home, drinking beer and passing out, night after night. "I dunno, Dad. They probably won't take me 'cause of my grades."

"Try it and see."

Kurt did and they took him! He couldn't believe it. He would have to take some remedial math which, he thought, was ironic, his father being a math professor. But what the heck? He'd give it a semester.

ROTC was required. He felt a little strange, almost the only white student marching, or trying to march, with all those black kids. But he made friends easily. They teased him some, white boy being the minority, but he formed relationships and bonds he still has today.

For some reason, he wasn't sure what, college clicked for Kurt. He started knocking down A's and B's, mostly A's. Some of it had to do with his high school sweetheart, whom he wanted to marry. She was a stabilizing force in Kurt's life, the rest of it was just wanting to make something of himself. He wanted to do something big. He wasn't sure what that was, he just knew it wasn't manual labor.

Interestingly enough, for a student who had to take remedial math upon entrance to college, Kurt took a shine to math and physics. Included with the math and physics was, of course, statistics and computer programming. He wound up getting a degree in math, which pleased his math-professor father to no end. Kurt chuckled to himself. He'd gotten D's and F's in math in high school, now he had a degree in it. Life could be funny that way.

Of course he had a military obligation to fulfill, which was no problem. He could take care of that in the National Guard. He liked the uniform and the idea of being an officer. It was all logic: Army, job, wife, kids, no going home every night and passing out in front of the television. He looked at his hands. He didn't want his knuckles to be swollen like Roscoe's.

He married his high school sweetheart, got a job with a big paper company in Des Moines, Iowa, and settled into the life of an upwardly-mobile White-Anglo-Saxon-Protestant—WASP.

It was at the paper company where he earned the title of a Six Sigma Master Black Belt—a person in charge of and training others to produce products that are statistically 99.99966% free of defects. He loved the math, statistics and logic. Applying it to manufacturing, with the help of the computer, he could analyze industrial processes, solve problems, and increase productivity. At his company, he brought down the cost of paper manufacturing and distribution close to 50%, a feat that brought Kurt a lot of recognition. He especially liked machines that broke down. He could analyze the data and predict to an uncanny accuracy when, and for how long a major piece of machinery was going to run before it had problems. The benefit to the company was enormous.

He taught his problem-solving and programming skills to others in the world-class company. It wasn't long before the company wanted to move Kurt and his family to corporate headquarters in Seattle, Washington. He was in the Iowa National Guard and could transfer to the Washington National

Guard. All the arrangements were made. He and his wife sold their home in Des Moines, bought another in Seattle, and were ready to move.

On his last day in Des Moines, he was checking in his gear at the armory. His wife and family were already in Seattle. There was a buzz amongst the other soldiers and they hardly paid attention to him on his last day. This hurt his feelings. They should be razzing him and playing tricks, like hanging a bucket of water over his locker. Instead they were in tight little groups, talking quietly, some apparently happy, others with a blank look on their face. Colonel Price was preoccupied, on the phone a lot and sending and receiving emails.

"Okay," Kurt could contain himself no longer. "What's going on?" he asked Price.

"Nothing. You're outta here. Good luck to you in Seattle. Teach them West Coast boys a thing-or-two. We grow corn in Iowa, not potatoes."

"Gotcha."

Kurt had his gear checked in and was on his way to his car. He stopped with his hand on the door handle. He couldn't leave like this. Something was going on. He went back in and could see Price through the glass in his office, talking with some other officers. Kurt tapped on the window.

Price cocked his eyebrows in a questioning manner.

Kurt motioned for Price to follow him to the locker room.

In the locker room, Kurt turned and faced his Colonel. "Awright, what's going on?"

Price turned around to see if anyone was within ear shot. There was no one. "You didn't hear this from me, it's classified. Awright?"

"Awright."

"Rumor has it the 451 is being deployed. Iraq."

A sick feeling hit Kurt in the gut. He turned white.

Price, noticing, said, "Hey, you're outta here. Seattle. The Sea Hawks. The Mariners. Get moving, soldier."

Kurt was on his way to the car again. He couldn't feel his feet on the ground. He felt like he was in a dream, walking on clouds. He called his wife in Seattle."

What's the matter, dear?" she asked.

"The 451's being deployed. Iraq."

"Wow. Dodged that one. Maybe you'll be safe with the Seattle Guard for awhile."

"I want to go with them."

"What?" She was incredulous.

"I want to go with them. The 451 means too much to me. What do I do?"

"What do you do? Oh, honey. We sold our house. We live in Seattle now."

"I know, I know. But the 451 is me. I love these guys. Just tell me what to do."

His wife was silent for a minute. He could hear her breathe out. "Whatever you do, this is your decision. You will live with it for the rest of your life."

He walked back into the armory and tapped on Price's window again.

"What is it this time, Captain Dingman?"

"I'm staying. I'm going to Iraq with the 451."

It wasn't all that easy. Kurt had been a safety officer with the 451. There were no positions open for safety.

But Colonel Price was going to find a place for a top-notch officer like Captain Kurt Dingman. "How smart do you feel, Dingman?" he asked Kurt.

"Smart, Sir?"

"Yeah, smart."

"Oh, I dunno. I feel more numb, if anything."

"Well, you better start feeling real smart real fast, 'cause I have one opening in Intelligence. You're going to be an Intelligence Officer."

"Intelligence, Sir? I dunno anything about Intelligence."

"Well, you're gonna learn, real damn quick."

"Yes, Sir."

With that, Captain Kurt Dingman was off for a crash course in Military Intelligence. They sold their house in Seattle and moved back to Des Moines.

The 451 went to Ft. Sill, Oklahoma for two months of training before they were shipped over seas to Iraq. They trained and trained and trained: convoy escort, route clearance, IED detection and removal. Much of the training they had to develop themselves because Ft. Sill was behind on the latest IED training. IED's were evolving so fast, from pressure-sensitive devices to remote control, through the use of wireless telephones.

Their equipment, like their Humvees, was not built to withstand IED detonation. Doors were non-existent or made out of canvas, and flooring was tin. Something called "up-armor" was applied, where heavy metal plates were cut and welded onto the existing framework, making the vehicles extremely heavy — heavier than what the suspensions were designed to carry. The vehicles were literally riding on their frames, making them hard to steer. A popular saying amongst the troops and the mechanics who were working on the vehicles was, "We will go to war with the Army we have," which was a direct quote from Secretary of Defense, Don Rumsfeld.

The 451 shipped off to Iraq on New Year's Eve, 2006. Rumor had it that the Army planned it that way so that the 451 would arrive in Iraq on January 1, 2007, New Years Day, thereby avoiding combat pay for December.

Refrigerator Box

When Dwight Jones was in the fourth grade in a little country school in Grover, Iowa, he was so disruptive and ornery the teacher brought a refrigerator box to school, cut holes in it for a door and windows, and put Dwight and his desk in it. And there he was to sit so he wouldn't bother the other kids.

Little Dwight sort of liked the box and the loneliness. He never did feel like he fit in with the other kids and, inside the box he didn't have to look at them, at their clothes that were finer than his, or at their lunches with sandwiches made from store-bought bread. Sometimes he didn't have a lunch, let alone milk money. Inside the box he didn't have to make excuses or pretend to be something or someone he was not. He was inside looking out.

Dwight's dad was an old hippie and alcoholic, moving from job to job. Dwight was conceived in the back seat of a Ford when his mother was 16. It was New Year's Eve, it was snowing, and Dwight's mother went out with the intention of having sex that night. She did.

They lived in a trailer outside of Grover, Iowa. The trailer did not have running water or a telephone. When Dwight got in trouble at school, which was often, the only way the teacher had of notifying his parents was by mailing a note. The Joneses lived at the end of a quarter-mile lane. When Dwight got off the school bus and checked the mail, if there was a letter from his teacher, he simply threw it away. If he was kicked out of school, which was also often, he wouldn't even tell his parents.

He simply walked down the lane to the school bus, but didn't get on. He spent the day fishing and hunting.

When he got a little older he learned how to make napalm and a crude triggering device from a Popular Mechanics Magazine. It was supposed to be for blowing up tree stumps. Dwight just doubled and tripled the ingredients. (This was his first foray into explosives, which would serve him well in the military.) By mixing gasoline with foam rubber in a gas can, and shaking it, napalm was the result. For a triggering device he used a spark plug wired to a 12-volt battery. He watched from behind a tree. When he touched the wires together there was a rather spectacular explosion and fire ball that caught a whole levy of the Mississippi River on fire. The fire department was called and Dwight hid in the woods for a day-and-a-half, eating mushrooms and crawdads before he went home.

At school, when he was a young teenager, he took a liking to a pretty little redheaded cheerleader. When she wouldn't give him the time of day, he set a time-delayed bomb off in her locker. He timed it so that kids would be in class and no one would get hurt.

The principal was really upset and the FBI was called in. Dwight was questioned, along with other kids, but nothing was ever found out.

Being a trouble maker, Dwight spent a lot of time in the principal's office, so much so that he had a permanent detention seat there--"Dwight's chair." The secretaries liked him and gave him money to go get them pop and sandwiches from the vending machines. The janitor, Mr. Wolf, liked Dwight too, and gave Dwight his keys to fill the pop machines. With the ring of keys in his possession, Dwight sent his buddies downtown to make duplicates. Pretty soon he had a key to every door in the school.

There were tunnels for heating ducts that ran under the school floors. Dwight and his buddies learned how to access the service doors using the duplicate keys, and crawl in under various classrooms. They would carefully open a trap door in the chemistry room or study hall and shoot spit wads at students. The pretty little redhead that had ignored him got one between the legs. She blamed another kid across the room, a jock, and Dwight and his buddies had a good laugh. The teacher or study hall monitor had no idea what was going on.

It was in PE class, which he hated, that he got the nickname, "Woodie." It was because he always had an erection. Dwight Woodie Jones he was called. If he even got close to a girl he would get an erection.

Because he lived in the country he took FFA. Not because his parents farmed (they didn't), but because he associated more with the farm kids, who, as a whole were more down trodden than the city kids. There were some rich farm kids too, who could be snobs, but as a general rule, the farm kids kept to themselves. All through grade school, it was always the town kids against the farm kids during recess and lunch-hour football and softball games.

Dwight also liked the blue jackets of the FFA students, and saw them as a counter to the town-kids' letter jackets. Grover was well known for its high school sports, and the "jocks" were a group of kids Dwight could not tolerate. He hated the way they walked (jock walk) and talked (jock talk), like sports was the end-all, be-all. "Put any one of them out in the woods for a week," Dwight thought, "and see how they survive." Dwight was at peace in the woods and around water, which for Dwight, was the Mississippi River.

He got in a lot of fights growing up. He lost about as many as he won. But Dwight was not afraid of getting whipped—he got plenty of that at home. He soon had a reputation as someone who would not give up. The jocks mostly left him alone, not wanting to soil their pretty letter jackets. They might be able to whip him, but they'd get hurt too, and they knew it.

The FFA teacher, who was in the National Guard, took a shine to Dwight and recognized his natural abilities and intelligence. The teacher gave Dwight a chance. The school had gotten their first IBM Personal Computers and assigned one to the FFA class. The computer sat in a corner, still in its boxes. The teacher, Mr. York (called Sergeant York by the kids behind his back), took Dwight aside, along with another student, Gerald, and gave them special assignments. "Dwight," he said, looking Dwight in the eye. "I want you to take that computer over there, learn how to use it, then teach the rest of the class how to use it. Gerald," he said to the other kid. "You build a computer table that it can sit on. Okay, guys? Get to work."

From then on, when Dwight came to FFA class, he went to the back of the room and worked with the computer. He sorta liked the isolation. It reminded him of the box he was confined to in country school. From inside he could look out and observe. The Computer had something called a Disk Operating System (DOS) and Basic Programming books. Dwight studied the books and took to them naturally. This was something he understood: logic, on-off, go, no go. And he had a natural ability to show the other kids how to use the computer.

Gerald made a fine computer table out of oak, with holes in the top for the computer cables.

It was mainly because of Mr. York that Dwight became interested in the National Guard. "Think about it, Dwight," Mr. York told him. "Serve your country, get a little education, make something of yourself."

When a recruiter came to the school, Dwight was attracted to him like a magnet. "You can sign up now, when you're 17, with your parents' permission, go to boot camp between your junior and senior year, then when you graduate, and you have to have a high school diploma, you will be in the National Guard. The Guard stays home and fights floods and fires, and does community service. The regular army fights the wars."

Dwight had been thinking about quitting school. The Iowa National Guard was the only reason he didn't. He liked the way Mr. York carried himself, with a little swagger and a confidence the other teachers didn't have. The National Guard might be okay.

His parents had no problem signing for him. They looked at it as a way of getting Dwight out from under foot. Besides, the National Guard stayed home.

So, Dwight went to boot camp and AIT between his junior and senior year of high school. He even had a chance to go to Germany for a few weeks, and he snatched it up, like a hungry boy in front of a hot meal. He had never known such freedom and discipline all mixed together. He was no longer in a box and could handle the barking drill sergeants and stifling regulations. Compared to his dad, drill sergeants were pussies. For the first time Dwight could see the future unfolding before him. It was all logical, like the computer, step by step, go-no-go.

When he returned to high school as a senior, he had been to boot camp, AIT, and Germany. No one messed with him. Even the jocks were in awe.

However, the principal, remembering Dwight's trouble-making days, had a trick up his sleeve. At graduation, Dwight was handed an unsigned diploma.

"This couldn't be," Dwight screamed inside. He had to have a diploma or the Guard wouldn't take him. He confronted the principal.

"Relax," the principal told him. "Come to my office."

Dwight went to the principal's office. The principal had a gleam in his eye and a signed diploma in his hand. He started to hand the diploma to Dwight but pulled it back. "First, gimmie them keys."

Dwight stared at him.

"I know all about those duplicate keys. You didn't fool me. Go get'm."

Dwight went home and got the keys, turned them over to the principal and received his diploma.

"One more thing," the principal said.

Dwight sighed, "What now?"

"I'm proud of you, boy. Go get'm."

Dwight was off and running. He took every course the National Guard had to offer. He ate, lived and slept the National Guard. He was a different man. He looked at himself in the mirror, in uniform. He liked what he saw. No one was going to out perform him, he could out-hustle anyone.

In the military, everyone hated nuclear, biological and chemical (NBC) training. They labeled it "NoBody Cares." It's because they didn't understand it. They had to wear protective suits that were hot, and face masks that were uncomfortable and fogged over. It was the unseen enemy: radiation, germ warfare, nerve agents. They would rather have an enemy that shot bullets, that they could see and fight and outmaneuver.

It was for this reason that Dwight signed up for NBC training: nobody else wanted it. It was an 18-week, very intense course, in Ft. McClellan, Alabama. McClellan had just built a brand new CDTF (Chemical Defense Training Facility) building that covered ten acres. Live agent could be and was used inside this facility for training purposes.

At one of the first main training events, with all the trainees suited up, with air-tight masks on and sensors in use, the trainees were to sound an alarm if they smelled the odor of bleach. Well, just mentioning the words "odor of bleach" almost made the students think they were smelling bleach, whether they actually were or not. It was a psychological thing, and Dwight was well aware of it, as were the other trainees.

Early in the 14-hour training exercise (this had to be realistic as possible, and exhaustion was realistic) Dwight thought he caught a slight whiff of bleach. But he ignored it, not knowing if his mind was playing tricks on him or not. An hour or so later, he thought he might be smelling bleach again. Once again, it was gone almost immediately, so he shrugged it off.

An instructor walked in and threw a vial of liquid against the wall smashing it, and spilling liquid. They watched it run down the wall. Their sensors started going off. This was it. This was real. There was live nerve agent and they were in the middle of it. They started their procedures of determining what the agent was, removal of the agent, and watching for signs of the effects of the agent on the soldiers.

As it turned out, it was a faux-live agent—one that had all the characteristics of the nerve agent, but was harmless.

After they went through the arduous procedure of decontamination, there was an hour for debriefing—talking about what happened, what went right, what went wrong, and how they could improve. They were all dead tired, from a 14-hour day of training.

The instructor who had thrown the vial against the wall walked in.

"How many of you smelled bleach?" he wanted to know.

As it turned out, they all had. But no one had said anything.

"You're all dead men. You know that. When an order is given that you are to sound the alarm if you detect bleach, it is just that—an order. This isn't an ice-cream social, soldiers. This is war!"

They were all looking at the floor, expecting that they might be busted or thrown out of the training school.

"Relax," the instructor told them. "You are the third class that's gone through this training course and third class that has failed to sound the alarm when they smelled bleach. Why? It's psychological. You don't know if what you're smelling is real or not. Do you really smell it, or is your mind tricking you?" (This instructor's language was clean because there were females in the class. He was having a hard time keeping his mouth in check, but the Army was changing. He wanted to use the "F" word so bad, but kept a tight lid on it.) "Take this to be a good lesson," he went on. "It's a damn good lesson for us as instructors, too. In war, especially in the type of warfare we are seeing now, terrorist warfare, the psychological factor is key. You don't know what is real and what is not. The best way to combat the psychological aspect is by training. Now get your dobbers up, we have a full day of training tomorrow."

It was a lesson Dwight would never forget.

It was in this class that Dwight met Francine. Since his bad experience with the red-head in high school, Dwight hadn't paid any attention to girls. He was too busy with the Guard. But Francine caught his eye, and she, his.

Like him, she wasn't any great catch, but when you're in

the military, far away from home, and lonely, and horny, what wouldn't attract you normally, became attractive. Fraternization between sexes in the military was forbidden. But the Army was changing. So what was forbidden was becoming, well, "Perhaps we can get away with it."

Actually, Francine approached Dwight. "You're from Iowa, right?"

"Yeah." Dwight had an immediate erection and was afraid she would notice it. He cursed himself for being so easily aroused.

"You're at the top of the class grade wise and participation wise," she went on. "I was wondering if you could help me study. I just can't get this Periodic Chart of the Elements."

Dwight was tongue tied. He could smell a whiff of perfume — something else that was not allowed in the military. It aroused him even more. He was afraid he was going to ejaculate in his pants.

"Maybe we could meet after chow, and you could go over some of this stuff?"

All he could get out was, "Yeah, sure."

They had sex on their first night. Dwight was a virgin and Francine recognized it immediately. She tried to guide him in, and he ejaculated in her hand.

Dwight was crushed and embarrassed. He thought he was spent.

Francine giggled. "It's okay. Let's go again. Let me help you."

Dwight had no idea that he could get off more than once. But here he was, erect again. This time, the sex was great. They even had a third time.

That did it. Dwight was in love.

Following the Nuclear-Biological-Chemical training, they

both had leave. Dwight took Francine to Iowa with him. He took her fishing, and pheasant hunting. Francine was from the south and had never seen a pheasant. She thought they were such pretty birds, and it was a shame to kill them.

Dwight was a crack shot, and was patient with Francine, showing her how to shoot fast, without really aiming, but pointing. Before long, she shot her first rooster pheasant and cried. "I can't do this. I can't kill. This bird is so pretty and deserves to be alive and free. Look, it's gasping."

Dwight didn't know what to say. He had hunted and fished all his life, and lived close to nature in the woods and on the river. He didn't give much thought to killing for food. He cautiously asked, "Can you shoot back if you're being shot at?"

"I don't know," she was sobbing uncontrollably. "I don't think so. I can't take another life."

Dwight was dumbfounded. Women weren't allowed in combat situations. Yet. But could he trust her in a NBC environment to do the right thing to save another soldier?

It was over between them. Francine didn't want anything to do with Dwight after that and he had fallen out of love with her. She went home to Alabama and they never saw each other again.

He did follow her career a little, to see where she was and what she was up to. He noted that she got out of the Guard the first chance she had.

Not Dwight, he was going for 20 minimum.

When 9/11 hit, Dwight was at a junk yard in Grover, in uniform, buying lead for duck decoy weights. His flip phone rang. It was his training officer. "Dwight, we're under attack. We're locking down Eastern Iowa—all highway and rail bridges, gas stations, the nuclear power plant at Blainsburg, and the one at

Harrington. We're issuing live ammunition, shoot to kill. This is it."

No one knew what to expect, who was the enemy? Bridges across the Mississippi had to be protected. The railroad bridge at Ft. June carried all the coal for Chicago. If it went down, Chicago had only an 11-day supply. There was credible intel that terrorists might try to blow up gas stations. Dirty bombs were a big concern.

Then the Adjutant General of the State of Iowa called. "Dwight, you're the Nuclear-Biological-Chemical person for Iowa. I need you to go to Carson City, to their big research lab and take whatever measures you need to secure it. They have some bad stuff there."

"Exactly what am I looking for, sir?" asked Dwight.

"I don't know, but you'll know when you see it. The university is cooperating fully. If terrorists get into that lab, it could be disastrous. We believe there's at least one, possibly two, sleeper cells in Carson City. In the student population alone, there is a major contingency of Middle Easterners—Iraq, Iran, Saudi Arabia. Immigration has lost track of a couple of them. Some of those pilots who hit the towers were Saudis. Get moving!"

"I'm on it, sir."

The first thing Dwight smelled when he walked into the research lab was bleach. He didn't have a chemical suit on, but all his internal warning buttons were sounding alarms. He found anthrax, bubonic plague, cholera, and more, all unsecured, sitting around loosely on lab tables, easy pickings for most anyone. The security was very lax, and there were so many door keys floating around, that the lab didn't know who had what.

Dwight changed all that real fast and filed a report with the Adjutant General detailing exactly what needed to be done and in what time frame. The lab still functions under the plans and security Dwight put in place.

He was the main Nuclear-Biological-Chemical guy for Iowa. It all went through him. And with 9/11, there was a lot of attention on NBC. It wasn't called "NoBody Cares" anymore. Everybody cared.

The bleach Dwight had smelled when he walked into the lab was a disinfectant the janitors had stored in a locker. "You're all dead men" echoed through his head and would be with him the rest of his life whenever he smelled bleach.

Females

There were no females in the National Guard before the Nineties, or very few. The few who were there were in non-combat positions like clerical, administration, or medical. Dwight was happy with that. Women, as far as he was concerned were a pain in the ass. Every unit that had a female, Dwight knew, was plagued with sexual harassment complaints and EEO bullshit. Women, for some strange reason, thought they should have equal opportunity for promotions and pay. Imagine that, when they couldn't even do the minimum requirement of push-ups, or carry as heavy a load.

If there was a female with a unit, there had to be two of everything: two porta potties, two bunk houses, two latrines. The piss tubes the men used in the field had to go, and the soldiers had to watch their language. They could no longer cuss like they were accustomed to, and they could no longer walk around naked. Having a female in a unit definitely put a crimp in the way things were done.

To top it all off, there could be no fraternization. Put a female in the middle of a group of horny soldiers out in the field, and it was nothing but trouble. Grab assing was common, as well as fights between men over a woman. There was even an occasional rape, or allegations of rape. Investigation of rapes, or sexual harassment, were always conducted by the NCO in charge—a man, of course. So the charges never went very far. But still, it was a nuisance, and time consuming. All soldiers had to go through hours and hours of stifling training on sexual harassment and EEO. Such a waste of time.

Dwight resisted having a female in his unit as long as he could. "Don't want'm, have no use for'm, they can ruin a well-oiled fighting machine."

The C.O. called Dwight and asked, "Why are you the only company in the battalion that doesn't have a female?"

Dwight knew he could talk bluntly and frankly with his C.O. "Because they're a pain in the ass, sir. They get in the way of me doing my job and obstruct a smooth running operation."

"I agree," quipped the C.O. "But here's the deal. You're the only company without a female, therefore you're my number one problem."

"Yes, sir."

"Get a female, and get one now."

"Yes, sir."

Dwight called his recruiter. "Fred, gimmie a female, fast. And I don't want a young, purdy one, neither. She needs to have been a full-time Army NCO and be mean as a snake. Wide as a barn would help, too. I don't want these young bucks crawling all over her, and our unit charged with sexual harassment. You understand, Fred?"

"Gotcha, Woodie."

A couple days later, Fred called back. "Got just the gal for you, Woodie. She was in the Army four years and was an NCO in administration. She's divorced with two kids."

"Ouch. Don't know if I like the divorced part. It might be open season on her, or her after every swinging dick."

"Can't have everything, Woodie. She's available and gift wrapped. Take her or leave her."

"Oh, okay. I'll take her. C.O.'s on my ass."

"One more thing, Woodie."

"What's that?"

"You need to get her to Camp Green in the morning for her induction physical. I'm gonna be out of town, and my back-up has the crud."

"You mean I gotta drive her to Des Moines?"

"That's the name of the game, Woodie. Ask me again I'll tell you the same."

Dwight met Virginia at the armory. He saw her from a distance. "Shit, she's good looking."

She stuck out her hand. "I'm Virginia Rappenecker. You must be Sergeant Jones."

They shook hands. Her hand was soft and warm and feminine.

Dwight melted on the spot.

On their drive to Ft. Green, which was long and boring (the four-lane highway hadn't been built yet) they wound their way through every little whistle stop. Dwight kept his eyes glued to the road, and didn't talk much. However, he did sneak an occasional sideways glance at Virginia's legs. They were long and slinky. Creamy, maybe.

Dwight spent the day at Ft. Green doing odds and ends of paperwork, while Virginia was being inducted. When he picked her up in the afternoon, she had passed her physical, raised her hand and was sworn in. She was an E5 in the Iowa National Guard. Dwight gave her a notebook and pen and told her to write down everything he told her. She was going to be his Administrative Assistant (which meant he could control her, or so he thought), she was to get fitted for her uniform, and there was to be no fraternization with the soldiers.

Virginia looked at him with a little smirk of amusement. She knew a tough nut when she saw one. But she also knew how to crack tough nuts—use a nut cracker.

On the ride home, Dwight loosened up some, and they made small talk. He asked her about her four year service with the Army. She asked him where all he'd been with the Guard and what his expertise was. She was impressed that he was NBC (Nuclear Biological and Chemical) certified.

"Isn't that Nobody Cares?" she asked, laughing.

"That's what some say."

"Well, I care." She had taken off her shoes because her feet hurt from her long day at Fort Green and she had been wearing heels. She raised her bare foot and put a big toe against Dwight's leg.

That did it. Dwight swerved into the nearest corn field, and they had passionate, outrageous sex. Six months later they were married—mainly so he could keep the other soldiers away from her. When Dwight went into the field, Virginia, as his Administrative Assistant and wife, went with him. Dwight was the only soldier in his unit who could have sex in the field—normal sex anyway. He was the envy of all his men. If he caught any of them lolly gagging around with Virginia, they had extra duty real fast.

No action was ever taken against Dwight for his "Fraternization." The Guard was changing.

Some said for the worse.

Promotion to E9

Dwight was on a training mission in Wisconsin. His unit had been in the field two weeks, blowing stuff up, building bridges and pretending there was a nuclear attack. Dwight, as well as his men, hadn't showered, shaved or changed clothes in over five days.

A jeep pulled up. It was Private Henshaw. They called him "Hen-Pecked Henshaw" because the Colonel used him like a punching bag. Henshaw walked up to Dwight and said, "The State Commandant is flying in tomorrow morning, and wants to see you."

Dwight turned around, looked at Henshaw, farted, and said, "Look, Hen-Pecked. If this is some sort of joke, I'm not in the mood."

"No, seriously, Woodie. The Commandant wants to see you."

"I s'pose he wants frequency cleaner, right?" (This is an old military trick played on Privates fresh out of boot camp. "Tell the Sergeant Major we need some frequency cleaner.")

"No. This is legit, Woodie. You are to shit, shine, shower and shave and be at the helipad at 0900. Savvy?"

"So help me God, Hen-Pecked. If this is a spoof, I'll tie your asshole in a knot and pour hot Ex-lax down your Chicken Little throat."

Dwight was at the helipad at 0900 along with the Colonel and his staff. They were all in line to meet the Commandant, with the Colonel at the head of the line. Dwight was at the end. Enlisted

NCO's were never invited to meet the State Commandant, except for the Sergeant Major. Dwight, as an E8, was an enlisted NCO. The others in line looked at Dwight like, "What's he doing here?" Dwight was wondering the same thing. He took a little aerosol canister of breath spray out of his pocket and sprayed some in his mouth. He offered it to the soldier beside him, but the soldier said, "Naw, I'm good."

The chopper landed, and before the rotors stopped, the Commandant stepped out, marched past the Colonel, who had his hand out, and right up to Dwight. Dwight saluted. The Commandant returned the salute and they both stood there cap brim to cap brim. Dwight could smell Dentyne on his breath. Dwight knew, you didn't fuck with a guy whose breath smelled like Dentyne. He would clean your clock.

"Jones!" the Commandant barked. "We got a hell of a mess in Bridgeport. That Battalion is fucked up. They are not combat ready, they have poor leadership, and they couldn't screw a goose if it was held for them. I've seen better morale in a whorehouse."

"Yes, sir."

"I've been watching you, Jones. You're one tough son-of-a-bitch. You do things by the book, and kick ass. I like that."

"Yes, sir."

"I want you to get them squared away, combat ready, looking sharp. I'm not fucking around. Those young Lieutenants need a prick to scare the shit out of them, and you're just the asshole to do it."

"Yes, sir."

"I'll give you three years. You do this and I'll make you an E9."

"Yes, sir."

So, Virginia and Dwight sold their house in Grover, and moved to Bridgeport. Since they would only be in Bridgeport three years, they rented a house instead of buying. Virginia's two boys, Robbie and Junior, didn't want to move, but went along reluctantly.

In the three years, Dwight did exactly what he was ordered to do. If soldiers were found shirking drill or sleeping in the barracks when they were supposed to be on duty, Dwight drummed them out of the Guard without hesitation, without listening to excuses. Needless to say, Dwight was not the most popular Sergeant on base. He didn't care. His battalion was to be combat ready and follow orders without hesitation, or they would be, "Outta here!"

It started with leadership. Dwight wanted all the NCO's and young officers to be pricks. Dwight didn't coddle anyone.

It worked. Dwight took the Bridgeport battalion from the lowest rating to the highest in less than three years. They were combat ready, looking sharp, and receiving awards—first in drill, first in preparedness, first in fitness. It was an amazing transformation and testimony to what can be done with good leadership.

But the promotion to E9 for Dwight didn't come. After the fourth year, Dwight was still an E8. Same with the fifth.

To make matters worse, the profit Dwight and Virginia realized from the sale of their home in Grover, $33,000, was subject to capital gain taxes unless it was reinvested. Since they hadn't bought a home in Bridgeport, because they thought they were going to be moved in three years, they were forced to pay the 22% capital gains tax. That really pissed Dwight off.

He held a terrible grudge against the Commandant for not giving him the promotion to E9 as promised. But then, Dwight knew, the Commandant was a good motivator, not a promise keeper. How he got to be State Commandant, Dwight wasn't sure. Ass kisser?

Dwight thought about beating the shit out of the Commandant, but knew better. The lack of promotion to E9 was a bitter pill for Dwight to swallow. But it was what it was.

Truth be known, the reason Dwight wasn't promoted to E9 was because of his weight. The Commandant had put in for Dwight's promotion but it was denied. The Guard had strict rules about promotions and physical fitness. Dwight's weight was out of sight. Dwight knew this, but preferred to put the blame on the Commandant.

It was at Bridgeport where Dwight met Lieutenant Dick Black and Sergeant Frank Blankenship.

Up-Armor

In Iraq, Warrant Officer Gordon, who was the chief mechanic for the 451 Combat Engineering Battalion, approached Dwight. "I don't know what to tell you, Woodie. We weld all this armor shielding on the vehicles to protect the soldiers from IED explosions, and it puts so much weight on the suspension that the vehicles lose 80-to-90 percent of their steering, which is very dangerous for the driver and occupants. It's a damned-if-you-do, damned-if-you-don't situation."

Dwight just stared off into the distance, like the answer was in the cloudless sky over Ramadi—in the heat. He didn't know it could get so hot, so he didn't waste words. "Those cocksuckers in Washington give us garbage for equipment and expect us to fight a Goddamned war. What the fuck are we supposed to do, Gordy? We can't send soldiers out there in armorless vehicles. They'd get blown to bits. So we up-armor, and it adds so much weight, the vehicle loses its steering, or a majority of it. Jesus-fucking-Christ, Rummy! 'We'll go to war with the troops and equipment we have.' You're fucking-A-right. I'd like to stick Rumsfeld's ass in one of these Humvees and see how he likes it. I'll bet we'd get the right equipment real Goddamned fast. The Marines have it, but not the Iowa National Guard!"

Warrant Officer Gordon spit a stream of tobacco juice as long as his arm, and wiped his mouth on his sleeve. "You want me to keep cut'n out steel and welding it on or not, Woodie?"

"Can you beef up the suspension, heavy duty shocks or struts, whatever they have?"

"They're already heavy duty, Woodie."

"Well, fuck it. Go ahead with the armor, I guess. We gotta do something, even if it's wrong."

Dwight watched a convoy go out. A helmet in one of the Humvees saluted him. It was Frank Blankenship. When Dwight had been with the Infantry Battalion in Bridgeport, he had helped recruit 17-year old Frank Blankenship into the Guard. Dwight had gone to the Blankenship home, with the Recruiter, met Frank's parents and persuaded them that the National Guard would be a positive experience for their son. It would be a place for him to mature (like Dwight himself had matured) while he was deciding what he wanted to do with his life. The Guard would train him and finance his college education. Dwight promised that he personally would look after their son—that no harm would come to Frank, that the National Guard (and here Dwight whispered a little prayer) stayed in country.

When Dwight's assignment with the Bridgeport Battalion was up and he returned to Grover, he talked, now 19-year old Frank Blankenship into transferring with him. "The Infantry is really a bunch of pussies," he told Frank. "It's the Combat Engineers who are real men. We do all the fighting when we clear the way, then the Infantry takes the credit. You'll learn more with the engineers. We build things. You'll learn a trade with the engineers instead of how to carry a gun and kick ass."

Frank was more than eager to follow Dwight's direction. He loved Dwight and wanted to be just like him. He would follow Dwight anywhere.

The same was true for Lieutenant Dick Black, who was also in the Humvee that passed Dwight. Dwight didn't recruit Lieutenant Black into the Guard, but Dwight sure as hell trained him on how to be an officer. In fact, Dwight was merciless when it came to giving Lt. Black "guidance." Like Lt. Dingman,

Dwight rode him like a cheap whore. If Black was going to be an officer, he had to grow up, and Dwight was going to make sure he did just that. An officer often had to make split-second decisions that could either save lives or kill the men they commanded. Dwight didn't pussyfoot around with Lt. Black. It's a wonder Black didn't hate Dwight, but he didn't. Black, as well as Dingman, revered Dwight Jones.

The Humvee also carried a gunner up on top, and of course, the driver. Dwight didn't like the way the Humvee tracked going down the road, if you could call it a road. It was more like a path in the sand. When the Humvee turned, the whole overloaded body shifted to one side, before the vehicle turned. When it turned back the other way, the body shifted to the other side, like a pendulum. Not good.

It was two days later when Dwight learned what happened. An IED exploded 20 meters in front of the Humvee Frank Blankenship and Dick Black were in. The driver, who was an experienced driver, swerved off road in loose sand, then tried to correct. He over steered, the body shifted, and the over-weight Humvee rolled, killing Frank Blankenship, and seriously injuring Lt. Black. The gunner and driver were hurt bad also.

Dwight had supplied the convoy with the safest route to follow. But like all routes, it was 80% safe. That 20% had cost the life of a soldier he was personally close to, Frank Blankenship, and injured three others. It was the 20% plus an overweight vehicle that killed them.

The war in Iraq became real for the 451 Combat Engineering Battalion. One man was dead and two others injured or fighting for his life.

Dwight was stunned and shocked beyond words. Frank, a

boy he had recruited and was like a son, was dead, and Lt. Black, who Dwight had trained, was fighting for his life.

A dark cloud came down over Dwight's head. He couldn't even reach up to grab a hold of something, because he didn't know where he was. Was this Iraq or a dream? He was in a fog. He could hear voices, but couldn't see who was talking.

Lieutenant Dingman was in almost the same state. The two were of no help to each other. Colonel Price asked them how they were. "Oh, we're fine," was all they would say. Men didn't talk to each other. They guarded their feelings like they were sacred, like if they let out how they really felt, it would be a sign of weakness.

Then Lt. Black died in Landstuhl, Germany, where he had been flown for medical treatment.

First Frank, now Lt. Black. Time stood still for Dwight.

He envisioned going home. What would he tell Frank's parents? "Oh, the coordinates I gave your son's convoy got him killed. Oops, sorry 'bout that. Or no, it was the heavy uparmor that made it difficult to steer the Humvee? I told you I would take care of him but I fucked up. I told you the Guard stayed in country. Now he's dead and it's my fault!"

Dwight didn't eat or sleep for three days. To this day, he still has nightmares about the incident. The Humvee is rolling over, and Dwight is trying to keep it upright. It flips and Dwight is pinned underneath it. He comes to as the Humvee lands on him, screaming in the night, his wife trying to comfort him.

Just another night with the never-ending war in his head.

It wasn't until the 451 started having some success with finding and removing IED's that they started getting factory produced armored vehicles, vehicles that were designed to handle the weight they were carrying. It was like the 451 had to prove themselves first before they got the right equipment to do the job they were sent to do.

Dwight looked at the new equipment and ran his hand along the steel reinforced sides and undercarriage. "I'm sorry, Frank," he whispered. "Please forgive me. Can I give you my life in exchange?"

Suicide looked like a good option for Dwight. In bed at night, lying on his back, he could see daggers circling around his head. He called these "dagger nights." He envisioned reaching up, grabbing one of the daggers and plunging it into his chest.

If he could have, he would have.

Interpreters

The two Iraqi interpreters were lying in plain sight on the desert floor, dead, beheaded, their heads lying close to their bodies, black tongues hanging out, eyes wide open — wild with terror — the bodies meant for the 451 soldiers to see, a statement of warning to all Iraqis who dared do business with the American infidels.

Dwight personally didn't trust the interpreters. But Mohammad, now lying dead in front of him, had that look that said, "You could have trusted me. I gave you my life." Dwight felt a longing and regret that he had misjudged Mohammad. Now it was too late.

Dwight wondered, "Was Mohammad like him — a man just trying to do his job, support his family? The culture in Iraq was so much different. Martyrdom was worshiped. In America life was precious.

"Jesus fucking Christ," he said to Captain Dingman standing beside him. "I can't do this anymore."

Dwight was in charge of paying the interpreters — crisp, new hundred dollar bills. Twelve. Twelve hundred dollars was a fortune in Iraq. It was enough to take care of the interpreters' families for months, a year even.

"Working for us cost him his life," Dwight said to Captain Dingman.

"Take it easy on yourself," Dingman told Dwight. "War sucks."

Dwight meticulously recorded the serial numbers on the

hundred dollar bills, which were in sequential order, so that Intel could trace the money and see how it was being used, where it was going and, maybe, why. Occasionally, Intel would find one or more of the hundred dollar bills on the body of a dead insurgent. What did that mean? Was an interpreter collaborating with the Insurgency, or had the money made its way through the Iraqi trade system and was now being used to purchase bomb making material? Dwight wished he knew. It was a reason to not trust the interpreters.

It was uncanny how the insurgents seemed to know when convoys were leaving and where they were going. All the insurgents had to do was bury their IED's and wait, cordless phones in hand. "One, two, three," detonate. Another one bites the dust.

When the Guard let the interpreters off to go home, they dropped them off way out in the desert to walk home, so that it wouldn't be known what they were doing and where they had been. Was it the hundred dollar bills that gave them away, blew their cover? Probably. Now here they were. Heads severed from their bodies, another clamp around Dwight's dry throat to add to the bad taste already in his mouth. Dwight felt like the life was being sucked out of him. He wanted to go home. This wasn't fun anymore. It wasn't his sandbox.

Most all of the male Iraqis who went to school knew English. Blackwater provided interpreters to the U.S. military — another reason to not trust the Interpreters. Dwight didn't trust Blackwater. As far as he was concerned they were mercenaries, hired by DC big shots who had stock in the company. Blackwater would fight for any organization that paid them the most money. And they were paid well.

Blackwater approached Dwight about working for them

when he was discharged. It would be a lot of money. Dwight could work for them for a couple of years and be financially set for the rest of his life. But was it worth it, selling his soul?

War was hell.

Arrangements were being made for one of the interpreters to escape Iraq and be given asylum in the U.S. when the 451's deployment ended. Dwight didn't know if this was a good thing or not. Was it building a nest of terrorists in the U.S., a cell, that could turn and become another 9/11, another World Trade Center going down?

Thoughts such as these troubled Dwight, and caused many sleepless nights. He didn't know who he could trust.

The headless bodies in the desert spoke volumes.

Call-to-Prayer, Sergeant Edward (Eddie) Beams

Colonel Price heard the Call-to-Prayer being blared over loudspeakers throughout the City of Ramadi, and a tingle went up his spine. Christianity and the Muslin Religion had the same roots, he knew. He also knew that after prayer was over, a rocket attack could be expected. It was like the insurgents finished their prayers and then set off their home-made rockets. "Allahu Akbar!" The rocket attacks usually did little harm. The military base was so large, and the rockets had little direction. Every once-in-a-while the insurgents got lucky, and a building was hit, some soldiers might be injured or killed, but generally the rockets did little damage.

The insurgents often fired the rockets from school yards, hospitals or mosques, knowing that the U.S. couldn't or wouldn't return fire--Rules of Engagement were strict on that. When the U.S. soldiers got to where the rocket had been fired, the insurgents would be long gone.

The insurgents also froze rockets in buckets of ice. When the ice melted, the rockets sank down, detonated, and the insurgents had already disappeared.

Price heard the whir of the rocket overhead and wondered where it would strike — probably somewhere in the desert doing little harm. This time there was a loud explosion, followed by secondary explosions. "What the fuck?" He threw on his gear and went to investigate.

Sergeant Dwight Jones heard the whir and the explosions also. They were so close, the door of his intelligence shack was blown open and one wall collapsed. He also put on his gear and went to the roof of his building to see what was going on. It looked like a 4th of July fireworks celebration. There were trailers shooting off in a zig-zag fashion, mixed with ground shaking explosions that shook the building he was standing on, and little rapid-fire firecracker sounds. Then he saw something he didn't want to see—a sight so horrific it would haunt his dreams to this day. There were a couple of soldiers on fire, screaming for their lives, rolling on the ground, trying in vain to put out the flames.

A 110 mortar had freakishly gone directly into the open hatch of a Paladin—a 155 mm, self-propelled howitzer tank, that had four marines in it. They had been trying to get coordinates on the location where the rockets were coming from so that they could return fire. The explosions and fireworks were from munitions in the Paladin that were "cooking off." It would go on for hours, leaving the Paladin a hunk of molten, smoldering metal.

Almost as troubling as the marines who were on fire, was that a nearby gazebo, that was used as a smoking shack by the 451st soldiers, was also on fire. Several of the 451 soldiers had been there smoking. One of them was Sergeant Edward (Eddie) Beams, from Grover, Iowa. He didn't even smoke. He was there shooting the bull with his buddies, and had the top of his head sheared off by shrapnel. He had just been home for Christmas before they were deployed. He was injured three days after he arrived in Iraq.

Candice Beams, Eddie Beams' wife, was at a Family Readiness Group meeting. Everyone was in a tizzy, and Candice couldn't figure out why. "What's going on?" she asked.

Don't you know?" one of the older ladies said, her eyes

gleaming because she had news someone else didn't."The 451 has been hit by rockets. It was all over the internet, until they shut it down. Massive injuries. We don't know who, how many, or how bad."

A sick feeling swept through Candice. She tried to calm herself. She thought, "Okay, there are over 500 soldiers in the 451. The odds of one of them being my husband is, let's see, one in..."

"Candice, the phone's for you." It was the older lady. The way she said it was too final, like if Candice didn't take the phone, she would be in trouble. The fact that the phone was a landline, instead of a cell phone, was also significant. Candice didn't want to take it, but held out her hand.

"H-h-hello?"

"Mrs. Candice Beams?"

"Y-y-yes."

"This is Major...."

Candice couldn't understand his name. But it was an older male with a smoker's voice."

"Your husband, Sergeant Edward Beams, has been injured. He is in route to Germany. You are to prepare for travel to an as-of-yet undetermined location. It will either be Frankfurt, Germany, or Washington DC, for either Andrews Air Force Base or Walter Reed Hospital."

The sick feeling intensified. "H-h-how is he?"

"We have no medical reports. You are to prepare for immediate travel. Do you understand?"

Candice felt light headed and saw stars. She was unaware that, at that moment, her husband was being resuscitated for the second time in the air over Germany. He was with his ancestors, Native Americans. They were telling him, "Not yet. Go back. Your time has not yet come."

He slammed back into his body.

The doctors were working frantically. They had Eddie mixed up with another 451 soldier who had been in the gazebo, Specialist Tim DePloeg of Erkson, Eddie's friend. Tim had an ear drum blown out, but could hear with the other ear. "No, no," he was telling the doctors. "I'm DePloeg, he's Beams." All their clothes and dog tags had been stripped or blown off at the explosion site.

Eddie Beams was perched above the surgeons and his body, looking down at them and himself. He felt a feeling of peace for himself but pity for the humans. They didn't know.

In addition to the top of his head being sheared off and his brain exposed, Beams' body was peppered with shrapnel and his right eye was gone. The doctors removed a chunk of skull and inserted it into his abdomen for safe keeping until he could get to brain surgeons wherever he was going. His body was swelling fast. I.V.'s with fluids and antibiotics, including penicillin, were injected into his body.

Back in Iowa, Candice Beams was in fight-or-flight mode. She had two kids to make arrangements for, and a new business, dog grooming and boarding, to button up. Her mother could take care of the kids, but it was the business she was worried about. They had just refinanced their house before Eddie was deployed, and built a new dog grooming and boarding building. How was she to make ends meet if she wasn't there? They could lose the house and business. But she had to get to her husband. And she didn't even know where she was going, Germany or Washington D.C.? The National Guard had little information about Eddie. However, they would send someone with her, to help get her to where she was going. His name was George Driller. He was in the 451 also, and they knew each other. At first Driller said he wasn't going because he was too close to Eddie. Candice told him, "No, you're going with me. I need someone to help me get to wherever it is I'm going. Please, George, go with me."

"Well, okay. But only until you get there. And then I'm coming back. I have things to take care of, too."

As it turned out, they were going to Walter Reed National Military Medical Center in Washington D.C.

When she first saw her husband, she couldn't believe it was him. He was about twice, maybe three times his size, and his face was unrecognizable, it was so swollen and wrapped in bandages, like a mummy. He was in an induced coma. The doctor was going through the list of medications. When he got to penicillin, Candice said, "Stop. You know he's allergic to penicillin, don't you? Where's his dog tags?"

"Everything was either blown off or taken off at the war zone."

"Well, it's a good thing you have him on a ventilator. Are you sure that's my husband?"

"We're doing the best we can, Ma'am." The doctor was young and obviously tired. There were so many injured coming in. Candice decided to give him a break.

At first she didn't know where she was going to stay. There was a military hotel at Walter Reed, the Malone House, for family members and some walking wounded. But it was full. They could put her in downtown D.C. but she didn't want to go there because she'd heard how dangerous it was. She could get mugged or worse just getting from downtown DC to the hospital. Magically a room opened up at Malone House.

After Eddie was taken off penicillin, the swelling went down and he started to slowly come around. The doctors were asking him questions. "What is your name?"

No response.

"Do you know where you're at?"

"Ah..."

"Who's the president of the United States?"

Eddie had false teeth and his dentures were missing—they were probably back in Iraq. The doctors could barely understand what he was saying. Candice held her ear close to his mouth and asked, "What did you say, Eddie? This is, Candice, your wife."

"My son's burffday is April twenty-turd."

So, they knew he was in there somewhere.

The doctors started weaning him off first one medication, then another. His cognitive abilities began returning. The doctors were amazed at what he knew, but also confused at what he was telling them.

Eddie mumbled, "They told me to come back. I wasn't ready."

"Who is 'they,' Sergeant Beams?"

Silence.

Candice, knowing her husband was part Native American, and of his beliefs, said, "I think he met his Great Grandparents when he died. They sent him back. He has work to do here on earth yet."

"That's fantasy, you know," the doctor said. "He was hallucinating."

"Oh?"

There was an officer at the hospital door. "I'm from the Med Board," he said. He was gruff and official. "These are Sergeant Beams' discharge papers. As his Power of Attorney, you are to sign them."

"Discharge papers?" Candice was flabbergasted. "You want to discharge my husband, after how many days since he was almost blown to bits?"

"He will be in the hands of the VA, Ma'am. Sign here."

"You can go to hell!"

After that, it was a game of cat-and-mouse. Every time she saw the man, she'd duck and hide. He was chasing down a lot of other people, too, trying to get them to sign discharge papers.

Candice called back to the Armory in Grover and talked to the skeleton 451 crew who were left behind. "What are they doing? It hasn't been 10 days since he nearly had his head blown off, and they're trying to kick him out?"

"Candice, relax. Eddie's not Guard now, he's Title 10, Active Duty. If he can't fight, he's a veteran, not a soldier."

"Veterans are treated like crap. He has a Traumatic Brain Injury — TBI. He needs care, not discharged."

For a Traumatic Brain Injury, she was told there were four places she could take Eddie: Tampa, Florida; Richmond, Virginia; San Diego, California; or Minneapolis, Minnesota. "What's the best?" She asked.

"Well, Tampa is the best. Maybe Minneapolis, second."

She wanted to choose Tampa, but it was too far from home. She had a family to take care of and a business to run. Without the income from the dog grooming business, they would lose everything — house, business, vehicles, tractors — everything. She chose Minneapolis because it was within driving distance.

They were put on a C-130 Transport to be flown to Minneapolis. They were the only ones on it. Candice looked around the big empty cargo plane, and said, "Can you believe this Eddie? We must be pretty special, huh?"

"Not really." Eddie was beginning to get his voice coordinated with his thoughts, along with his sarcastic sense of humor. "It shows how bad they want to get rid of us. You must've put'm through the wringer, Candice."

"Not really. They ain't seen nothing yet."

When they landed, they were met by another officer before disembarking. "These are Sergeant Beams' discharge papers. You are to sign them before you get off."

"I'm signing nothing," Candice said. "I told them back in DC. He was blown to bits in the military, the military can take care of him."

"Well, then, you're not disembarking. This ship is headed back to DC in 30 minutes. Sign, or you're going back to DC."

"Are you serious?"

There was a look in the officer's eyes and a set to his jaw that said he was dead serious. She signed the papers.

The officer seemed relieved. "You're the VA's problem now, Ma'am."

At the VA hospital in Minneapolis, she met with the surgeon. He was young and nervous. "How many TBI surgeries have you performed?" Candice wanted to know.

"I've done enough."

"That's not what I asked. I asked how many."

"Two. I've done two."

"Two! You're not touching my husband. I've watched too many TBI's go into surgery walking-and-talking, and come out a vegetable. I was told in DC that his surgery would be done at Walter Reed where they do two before they even have breakfast. I want to go back to Walter Reed."

"That's quite impossible, Ma'am"

"Impossible? I'll show you impossible."

Candice started calling State Representatives in all the surrounding states—Minnesota, Iowa, Wisconsin, Nebraska,

Illinois. She raised so much hell that a delegation of politicians was formed to go into the VA Hospital in Minneapolis to see how veterans were being treated after they left Walter Reed. Of course, Eddie, being able to walk and talk, called a "Walkie-Talkie," was one of the "veterans" they talked to. He had his teeth back now, they were specially flown from Iraq, and he was prepared. Candice couldn't believe it, and was so proud of him. She heard her husband tell a woman Representative, "I'll put it this way, Ma'am. My wife runs a dog grooming and kennel business back in Iowa. We treat dogs better than the way we're treated here."

The woman representative made a note.

Eddie and Candice were put on another empty C-130 and sent back to Walter Reed. Eddie quipped, "This is becoming routine, Candice. You musta really raised some hell."

"No, it was you, Eddie. You told'em, by golly."

Eddie had just come out of surgery and was groggy. Iowa Governor Tom Vilsack and his wife came in. "Is there anything we can do for you?"

Candice spoke up. "When we were in Minnesota they told us about the Injured Military Grant that they have there, to help pay bills, like mortgages and put food on the table. Why don't you get something like that going in Iowa?"

That's how the Iowa Military Grant got started. It was nick-named the "Eddie Beams Grant"--$10,000 awarded to soldiers or the families of soldiers who were injured in a war zone. Candice didn't apply for the money, someone else, she didn't know who, applied for them. The money saved their home and business and would prove to be both a blessing and a stain on the Beams' family.

Candice and Eddie's parents were lodged at the Malone House when he was at Walter Reed for the second time. It wasn't a very safe place. When one wife was raped while walking from the Malone House to the hospital at night, Candice began staying over at the hospital until they kicked her out. She also started carrying a knife in her purse.

When they moved Eddie from ICU after surgery, they moved him to the General Medicine floor. Candice knew this wasn't right. None of the nurses knew how to take care of him. She asked one of the main nurses, "Will you promise me that you are going to turn him every two hours like you're supposed to?"

"Yes, Ma'am."

"Don't blow smoke up my butt. If you say you're going to do it, will you please do it?"

"Yes, Ma'am."

Candice left to get a couple hours of sleep. When she came back, Eddie hadn't been turned once in four-and-a-half hours, and his medicine was still sitting on the counter, untouched. He had to be turned every two hours. There were bed sores all over his body, like it was a pin cushion. After that, between Candice and Eddie's parents, there was someone with him 24/7.

Walter Reed only allowed two people to stay at the Malone House and to be registered visitors of a patient. However, since Eddie was so close to death, she talked them into allowing both parents to stay and visit. That meant a spouse and two in-laws sharing the same room, for four-and-a-half weeks, which is something that should never happen. She could hear them belching, snoring, groping each other and farting in the night, and they could hear her talking in her sleep and grinding her teeth. Then there was the problem of getting dressed and showering.

Although conditions were strained at best, they made it work, because of Eddie.

Eddie's mother was in poor health and had difficulty getting around. So Candice found herself caring for not only Eddie, but his mother. Women are always the caregivers. Eddie's father seemed incapable or not to care about his wife. But, Eddie, yes.

In the middle of the night, when Eddie was on that General Medicine Floor, there was a floating nurse who came in. She was looking at him, and flipping through his chart, shaking her head and mumbling. She said to Candice, "He's not supposed to be here. He needs to be down on Ward 57."

"What's Ward 57?" Candice asked.

"That's for traumatic brain injury. That's where he needs to be. He has no business being here. They have no idea how to take care of him here."

Uncharacteristic, Candice was tongue tied.

"You didn't hear this from me," the nurse continued, "but you get on the phone first thing in the morning and you start screaming, and I mean screaming!"

Now Candice was in her element. She started down the list— CEO of Walter Reed, Chief Surgeon, Head of HR—and wasn't getting anywhere. So she started threatening. She told the head nurse, "I can make two phone calls and get the reporters in here, Washington Post and New York Times. Do we need to do that? I will."

"That won't be necessary."

12 hours later he was moved. They had one bed open in the Traumatic-Brain-Injury Ward. He started getting better almost immediately. He was finally with people who knew how to take care of his injuries. It was a huge difference. But Candice still watched everything like a hawk.

There was a mother whose son was an amputee. She was from Pennsylvania. Candice and she would take turns. If they had to step out, they'd watch the other person's soldier to make sure everything was taken care of.

For the most part, everybody had each other's back. It didn't matter what branch of service they were in. The families made sure everybody was taken care of.

The DOD medical staff was perfect. They knew their stuff and how much they could and couldn't do. The civilian medical staff was deplorable. Candice couldn't figure out why. It was more of an attitude toward the soldier, like, "You got yourself into this mess, you can get yourself out, and you're National Guard, not a real soldier." She did not want them taking care of Eddie.

Larry Jordan came in from the American Legion in Des Moines. A whole group came to DC and the Walter Reed Hospital. It was Memorial Day and Eddie was presented with the Purple Heart by Secretary of Defense Donald Rumsfield. Eddie wanted his Commander, Colonel Price, to present it to him, but the 451 was in Iraq. Mr. Rumsfield was very sincere. He was there for almost an hour talking to Eddie. You didn't see a lot of politicians doing that, not for that length of time. A lot of people gave Rummy a bad rap for his "We'll go to war with the troops and equipment we have," statement. But unlike a lot of politicians he was there for the troops.

There was a lot of brass coming and going, and Candice began to be recognized. When she walked down the hallway, people would say, even military bigwigs whom she had no idea who they were, "How you doing, Mrs. Beams?"

She was fast on her feet: "Am I smiling?"

They would laugh and give her a thumbs up.

She had learned to scream. Most people think that when you're sent to the Walter Reed Hospital in Washington DC, it's the end-all, be-all. It's not. The military will discard anyone, anytime, anywhere if they feel it's necessary and they think they can get away with it.

Is it possible to get Post Traumatic Stress Disorder (PTSD) or Secondary PTSD from being in a place like Walter Reed? Candice Beams believes so. It is definitely not a place for children, so she was glad she had her mother to care for her kids at home. The smells, the sounds, the sights, the violence, plus the concern for one's soldier, could drive anyone over the brink.

But they were also fortunate they were at Walter Reed. The hospital took the injured, who were able, as part of their therapy, out to different sites. They were taken to the Pentagon, and to places most people didn't get to see, like the lawn where the terrorists crashed the jet airplane. There was a memorial for all the people who had lost their lives at the Pentagon. Candice read through the names, and the last four weren't American names. She asked the Airman who was giving the tour whose names those were. He said, "Those are the terrorists who took down the plane."

"Are you serious?" she asked. "Why would you put their names on this memorial?"

"It's for historical purposes, Ma'am."

"Do you realize you just let the terrorists win? Their names are in stone!"

Not only was Candice upset but so was everyone else on the tour, especially the walking wounded.

She was standing in a little alcove. All of a sudden she couldn't breathe and her heart was pounding. There was something about the place that felt eerie. "What happened here?" she asked.

"That's where the plane came in, on the spot where you're standing.

They were taken next to the Vietnam Memorial. It was winter time and it was snowing and freezing. She put her hand on the wall. It was hot. "Do you heat this wall?" she asked.

"No, Ma'am. It's black and holds heat."

"In the winter on a cloudy day and it's freezing?"

The tour guide shrugged his shoulders.

In the Malone House, they buddied up wounded warriors as roommates, those who still needed medical care but didn't have family members there. They were supposed to take care of each other. They were on the TDRL—Temporary Disabled Retired List. They had to show up for formation everyday even with limbs blown off and in wheel chairs. If they didn't they were written up.

There was one guy they called Spider Man. He was up on the roof all the time, and wouldn't come down for formation. The brass could never catch him to write him up. Whenever the walking wounded stood outside in formation, they would look up and there Spider Man would be, on the roof, looking down at them.

One morning when they looked up, Spider Man jumped to his death.

No roll call was taken that day.

Candice was instrumental, through the Wounded Warrior Project, to mandate that if the soldier was suffering from diagnosed PTSD, which the majority of them at Walter Reed were, they couldn't be written up for insubordination or not following orders. Also, the Med Board could no longer talk to a soldier with a traumatic-brain-injury for one year after their injury. Candice was pushy, yes, but she got things done.

When Eddie and Candice got home to Grover, it took them several days to get settled in. Eddie needed care 24/7, the kids were suffering from not having their parents home, the house and barn where Candice did the dog grooming and boarding were a mess, and there was a stack of bills a foot deep.

Angela, Eddie and Candice's daughter, had been born prematurely. She was small and had cognitive and mental issues. When Benton, Eddie and Candice's son, was one year old, Angela dropped Benton on his head, fracturing his skull and causing a brain bleed. So both Eddie and his son had a traumatic-brain injury, which was all Candice needed, two family members with TBI.

The VA in Rochester called, a woman nurse. "We think Mr. Beams may have a traumatic brain injury."

"You think?" Candice lost it. "Jesus Christ! He had the top of his head blown off, he has a steel plate in his skull, one eye is gone and he can barely see out the other. He has seizures, he can't feed himself, he wears Depends and screams in his sleep. You think he has a traumatic brain injury? Do you even read his file?"

"I'm sorry, Ma'am. I had no idea..."

"We have just gone through six weeks of hell at Walter Reed. Are you people here going to be of any help at all? This man laid down his life for this country."

"He will be our first Iraqi poly-trauma veteran. We intend to give him the best care in the world."

Candice was skeptical. "Really? What's that?"

"Well, let's see."

Candice could hear her flipping through pages.

"We have him scheduled for speech therapy, occupational therapy and voke. A neurologist will see him, as well as a neuropsychologist, psychiatrist, psychologist, an eye specialist, and VA Counselor. Then there's the adaptive equipment specialist. I think that's everything."

Overwhelmed, all Candice could think to ask was, "What's voke?"

"Voke? That's vocational rehabilitation."

"Oh, of course. Let's not forget that one."

"We'll need him here three days a week."

"How am I supposed to do that?"

"You can put him on a shuttle. It leaves at 5:30 in the morning and he will need to be here all day."

Candice hit herself in the forehead with the heel of her hand. "Eddie needs care 24/7. I have two special needs kids and a business to run. It's an hour drive to Rochester. Can we find therapy closer?"

As it turned out, some of the therapy could be accomplished at Erkson, which was only half-an hour away, instead of an hour. He still had to meet with the poly-trauma specialists in Rochester once a month, but the Beams' family managed. Eddie was home.

Everyday when Eddie woke up he'd say, "Why did I live and those other guys die? Why am I alive? There must be a reason."

"You're to help others, Eddie," Candice told him. "You're to tell your story to other disabled veterans, just like yourself. There is hope. There's still something you can do even though you can't walk. You're adaptable. You're a Beams, Eddie. You don't give up."

And that's how Raccoon River Outfitters, in Hurds County, Iowa, got started. He teamed up with a retired military person,

Charlie Harris, and others to create a place for disabled veterans where they could hunt and fish and drive four-wheelers, enjoy nature and rub shoulders with others just like themselves. Many of them were suffering from PTSD. Peer-to-peer contact is some of the best therapy.

They took veterans fishing on the Boundary Waters between the United States and Canada. They showed veterans that anything they could do before they were disabled, they could still do, through adaptability. Raccoon River Outfitters had a "disabled person," who had been born without arms, come in and talk to the veterans. The armless person could do anything a person with arms could do, only using his feet, like drive a car, do a brake job on the car, fish, hunt, shoot a gun, raise a family, go to college, anything they wanted to do. All they had to do was go after it and not give up. And even giving up was okay. Because sometimes, giving up for a period of time was what was needed, so that they could revisit the goal later when they were more ready. When the pupil is ready, the teacher will appear.

Eddie got involved with the Navajo Indians in the Southwest and, because of his Native American blood line, and disabled veteran status, was allowed to participate in the Sweat Lodge Ceremony. Water was poured on the hot rocks and steam arose and was trapped in the animal hide-and-bark covered hut. He was there for two days and was ready to come out, thinking it had been a failure. A figure appeared to him in the steam. Eddie thought it was one of the Sweat Lodge organizers coming to tell him that his time was up. Instead, the figure, that appeared to be an old man dressed in a buffalo robe and eagle feathers, pointed his finger at Eddie and told him that he was to go back, that his mission was not complete, that there was work to be done.

On the outside, Eddie asked the event organizer who the old

man was, that he was just like the person he met when he died in the helicopter over Germany.

The event organizer turned white as a sheet. "That was your Great Great Grandfather. Listen to him. You are not ready to be with them. Your work is not done."

"What is my work?" Eddie asked.

"You are to help wounded warriors."

Eddie always said that the National Guard saved his life. Which is sort of ironic because the Guard eventually took his life. He'd been an alcoholic before he joined, or a drunk. He'd been in and out of jail several times and couldn't hold a job. When he joined the National Guard, on a whim, and on a bet with another drunk, he straightened up almost immediately. He loved the discipline and the pride and the clear path to advancement. Go to this school and get this promotion, do this, get that. There was no more flying blind like he had been doing.

The Guard put him into heavy equipment operation which he loved. Bulldozers, road graders, cranes, explosives, bridges — he couldn't get enough of it. In fact, it was because of the heavy equipment training in the Guard that he landed his dream job in the civilian world: heavy equipment operation for the DOT. He had tried several times to get on with the DOT but didn't have enough experience. Once he had the heavy equipment training in the Guard, several counties were bidding for him at once. He went with Fullbright County.

When he met Candice, he told her that he had formerly been an alcoholic, and she didn't believe him. He was too squared away. She'd always heard that once-an-alcoholic-always-an-alcoholic — one drink away from a drunk — that sort of thing. Eddie didn't attend AA meetings and he wasn't in any kind of addiction recovery program that she could see. She wondered if he was a ticking time-bomb. Ironically, once again, that would be exactly what happened, a bomb, only in the literal sense of the word.

Eddie always maintained that he would have been dead from alcoholism if it hadn't been for the guard. So, in a sense, the Guard kept him alive for another few years.

After Eddie was home, very few of the 451 Engineering Combat Battalion came around to see him. Albeit, the bulk of them were still deployed in Iraq. Even after they returned home, very few came to see Eddie, which hurt both Eddie and Candice. Candice would run into some of the 451 guys at Walmart or around town, and they would ask, "How's Eddie?"

She would say, "Well, you could stop by and see for yourself, you know. Eddie loves for the 451 to stop in."

"Oh, we just hate to see him like he is."

Candice was so flabbergasted she was at a loss for words—which indicates how upset she was.

Eddie loved and craved for his Guard buddies to stop by. There were a couple of guys who routinely came by to take Eddie out to dinner, and Eddie so loved and looked forward to those trips out. But most of the others were few and far between.

When the 451 returned home from Iraq there was a big public reception for them in the Grover Armory. Ribbons, medals and citations were handed out at this event. Eddie wanted so badly to be able to stand at attention with the rest of his battalion. However, he wasn't able to and had to be held up by two of his friends. He listened to the band playing and the speeches. "God, I love this country," he whispered to his two friends holding him up.

There was a banquet for the 451 in Grover. Eddie was bound and determined he was going to walk into the banquet without assistance. He worked and worked on his walking and was able to accomplish his goal of walking into the banquet without help. His friends congratulated him and told him how good he looked and how good it was to see him. Candice was close by, of course, in case her husband needed help.

Colonel Price walked up to him. "Sergeant Beams, it's so good to see you. How you doing?"

"Oh, I'm doing fine, Colonel. But I miss the action. You?"

"Fit as ever, but the action could slow down a little, as far as I'm concerned." Colonel Price looked him up and down, noting the scar across Eddie's forehead where the metal plate had been inserted, one eye with a patch over it, and Eddie's obvious effort to stand erect. "Tell me, Sergeant Beams, if you had to do it over, considering all you've been through, and all you've seen, would you change anything?"

Eddie didn't hesitate, almost as if he was prepared for this question and had rehearsed his answer. "You know, Colonel, I wouldn't change a thing. I'm proud of my country, proud of the service I've given it, and willing to do more if called to do so."

Candice was standing close by and heard Colonel Price. She stuck out her chin, looked Colonel Price in the eye, and with one hand on her husband's shoulder, she said, "Ask ME that question."

Colonel Price knew when to keep his mouth shut.

Later in the evening, after they had eaten and were having drinks, a soldier, whom Candice didn't know, walked up to her. "How's that $10,000 treating you?" he asked.

Candice's mouth dropped open. Once again, she was so flabbergasted, she was at a loss for words. Her mind said, "If you only knew," but her mouth wouldn't work, like she was in a dream.

She never went to another "social" event for the 451.

It was a constant fight with the VA. Ever since Eddie had been injured it was one fight after another for Candice, and she was tired of it, worn out. When the VA informed her that Eddie's therapy was going to be discontinued, that he was, "As good as he's going to get," she blew a gasket.

"Are you shitting me?" she screamed. "Just this morning he said, 'It's a good day to die.'"

"I'm sorry, Mrs. Beams. Calm down. Where he is at is where he is going to stay for the rest of his life."

Candice grasped at a straw. "But you have to do maintenance therapy." She had no idea if they had to or not.

That stopped the VA Rep in her tracks. She didn't know either whether they had to do maintenance therapy or not, but this woman, Mrs. Beams, seemed to know what she was talking about. "Okay. I'll tell you what we'll do. We'll have the counselors see him once a month to determine how he's doing. If he slides backwards, we'll inpatient him. If he improves over where he is now, we'll cut him loose. Deal?"

"I'm not making deals. What I will do is call Governor Vilsack. I have his private phone number."

"Hold on now, Mrs. Beams. That won't be necessary. We'll look after your husband. No need to get the governor involved."

Something deep inside Candice told her Eddie wasn't going to live for 10 years following his injury. So by golly she was going to make life as comfortable and as fun as possible and as meaningful for her husband as she could. There was a non-profit retreat in Idaho (she had found it on the internet) that took wounded veterans in and let them drive snowmobiles. Half of them were blind, but it didn't make any difference. "Damn the right-of-way!" A volunteer would sit behind them and tell them which way to turn—"Left, right, straight, faster!" It was a scream. And the men-and-women wounded warriors loved it—the fresh air, the snow hitting them in the face, the feel of an engine between their legs, the smell of exhaust.

And the American Legion in Fullbright County took disabled veterans out turkey and deer hunting, fishing and mushroom hunting, even sky diving. The Legion would pack the veteran and a hunting blind on a four-wheeler and drive deep into the timber of Fullbright County. The veteran would get the thrill of calling in a gobbler, or watching a buck follow a scent trail to their blind. They used crossbows if necessary, or black-powder rifles, anything to get the wounded veteran in position to take a shot. During slow times of turkey hunting, they would mush-room hunt—morels being almost as fun as a gobbler, and more tasty!

One veteran even took down a near trophy buck with a cross-bow. With the help of his guide, they measured the rack and entered it into Pope and Young—a record keeping organization for racks taken by bow. It was one of the bigger racks taken in Fullbright County that season by bow or shotgun. Considering Fullbright County has the largest deer population in Iowa, that's saying quite a bit. The veteran couldn't have been more pleased, and the mounted deer head now hangs above his fireplace, memories of a great hunt.

Eddie had been fishing at Raccoon River Outfitters. He loved it there. The small mouth bass and crappies had been hitting hard. There were two things he couldn't get enough of: fried fish and mushrooms.

He'd left a trailer there and needed to go back to get it. He had a drivers license now and could drive as long as he hadn't had a seizure in six months. He needed to go back to Raccoon River and pick up the trailer and bring it home for the winter.

Something didn't feel right to Candice, but she let it pass. Eddie was doing fine by himself on short road trips. She had no cause for worry. Raccoon River Outfitters was about 35 miles from their home at Grover. He should be able to handle the drive by himself. Charlie Harris would be there to help him hook up the trailer.

As it turned out, Charlie got caught up in something else and wasn't there when Eddie arrived. Charlie found him on the ground face up, in the woods where he belonged, a smile frozen on his face. He died of a brain aneurysm.

He had made it six years.

Candice spent two weeks as an inpatient in mental health— Secondary PTSD. She knew she'd given Eddie everything she had, and then some. She'd fought for him when he couldn't fight. But there was a nagging feeling that if she'd just done a little more, that if she hadn't let him go after that trailer, that if she'd been a better wife, a better lover, he'd still be alive. It helped that she had the government to turn her frustration on.

Eddie's picture is on the Freedom Rock for Fullbright County. Let us never forget. Let us never forget any veteran of the United States Military.

Purple Heart

The explosion turned them upside down. Pinned to the ceiling of the Humvee, Medic Chris Mitchel was upside down and couldn't move her legs. She could move her arms, but not her legs. She tried to cover her ears to stop the ringing, but she had on noise suppressors and realized the ringing was coming from inside her head. Everything was black, pitch black.

She felt for her flashlight, pinned to her blouse, found it, and fumbled for the switch. Her thumb hurt real bad, like it had been smashed in a car door. She could feel movement starting to return to her legs. It felt like when she was a little girl, in bed in the middle of the night, having to pee, but not wanting to get out of bed in the cold, dark night, not knowing what was out there.

A moaning at her side let her know that SFC Gorkin was at least semi conscious.

A pain shot through her thumb, but she tried again, disregarding her broken thumbnail, and was able to switch the flashlight on. There was so much dust and sand and grit swirling in the air inside the Humvee that it was like a blizzard, a sand blizzard. An acrid smell, that got in her mouth and burned her eyes, let her know it was cordite, one of the many ingredients used in an IED cocktail. She wondered if there would be a secondary explosion, like in an earthquake, or if her light would draw the eyes of a waiting sniper, that is, if she could make it outside of the overturned Humvee.

She felt Gorkin move his leg. She trained the light on him and saw blood pumping out of his neck like a geyser. She tore at the Velcro on the front pockets of her jumpsuit. She found a large compress, ripped it open, and put it over Gorkin's neck and throat. She then pulled his right hand up and placed it over the compress. "Hold it there," she told him. His large round eyes, caked with dirt, let her know he understood.

She shown the light around the inside of the over-turned Humvee. The driver was fumbling for the escape hatch and the gunner was holding him up. At least they were mobile, she told herself. She had to get outside the vehicle and do a triage of the injured, sniper or no sniper. Her legs seemed to be working now. She had a huge gash across her right thigh that for some reason wasn't bleeding. Caked in dirt? she wondered. It didn't matter. She had to get to the injured.

Twenty meters from the Humvee was the charred body of Specialist Herman Stein, his clothes mostly burned off him. But amazingly, he was conscious. He was looking straight up at the night sky, a slight smirk on his blackened face, like he was looking at God.

"Herman, Herman, can you talk?" she asked.

He coughed and said, "Is today the day I get my Purple Heart, Mitchel?"

"Would you cut that shit out, Specialist Stein? Where do you hurt the most?"

There was no response. She shown the light in his eyes. His eyes were glazed over, but still looking up. He was gone.

Specialist Herman Stein was one of the first soldiers she met when they deployed to Iraq. He had been with another battalion, so this was his second deployment. He had signed up with the 451 knowing they were deploying. He wanted to go back. For what reason, Chris didn't know.

Without hesitation, when they first met, Herman looked her up and down and bluntly asked, "You wanna hook-up tonight?"

like he had no doubt asked countless other female medics and admin staff. It was a question asked as easily as if asking if he could pick up a gallon of milk for her since he was going to the PX anyway.

Chris knew exactly what he was asking and was shocked by his audacity, but also a little flattered. She needed to know she was attractive to men. "Uh, no thanks," she told him. "I'm a newlywed."

She saw the wheels spinning in Herman's head. He was asking himself, "Newly wed and wanting to be faithful, or newly wed and horny but not wanting to show it?" So she continued with emphasis, "I don't mess around. I said my wedding vows and I intend to keep them."

From then on they were fast friends. He respected her, and she looked after him like a wild brother who needed looking after. Which he did.

Herman Stein was a free-wheeling, practical jokester, putting rubber snakes in soldiers' sleeping bags; an excellent impersonator of higher ranking brass, especially stiff-necked sergeants; and a stand-up, improvisational comedian who could keep the troops in stitches during hard times, which was most of the time.

Everywhere they went, every mission, if there was sand, and there always was, Herman would lay down and make a sand angel like a little kid in the snow. After making the impression, he would take a can of orange spray paint, which the military had plenty of, and spray paint, "Herman Stein Was Here," in the sand impression, a prime example of an over-stuffed ego, or so Chris thought. "Look at me, I was here. Like Killroy."

Who gave a rat's ass?

And he had quirky political views, or maybe they were more poignant and blunt than quirky. His views certainly weren't patriotic. "Why are we here?" he would ask, even to the top brass.

"If you wanna win this god-damned war, draft us for the fucking duration, like they did in World War II, and I'll betcha my asshole to your mouth, we'll have this baby cleaned up in no time. You give us one-year hitches, all we're doing is keeping our heads down for one year. Next battalion in. At the rate we're going, this is gonna be a twenty year war with no victory, and an embarrassment to the U.S."

Chris couldn't argue with him.

Then, like Herman had a split personality, he would switch, almost in mid-sentence, and be the arch-typical class clown—mimicking, impersonating, telling jokes—keeping the troops entertained. But like all class-clowns, Chris suspected, it was really a cover for a sensitive, hurting person trying to hide a bundle of troubled feelings.

But not to Chris. With Chris he was honest, to the point of her wanting him to shut up. She was bothered by what he had to tell her—things like, "I know I'm not going to make it home alive from this tour. It's just a feeling I have. I have a little girl my mother is taking care of. I want you to visit her and tell her what her father was like, really like, no white wash."

Just that morning, before they left on the mission on which he was killed, he had told Chris, "I think today is the day I'm gonna get my Purple Heart."

"What the fuck is it with you, Stein?" Chris tried to talk like the male soldiers, and some of the females, so they would include her in their little ring of confidants. Trust went a long ways when it came to emergency medical treatment in the field. "You got a freaking death wish or something?"

That stopped Herman in his tracks, but only for a moment. She could see the wheels spinning in his head again. "Death wish maybe, Mitchel. But me thinks it's more like survivor's guilt."

Chris didn't know what all happened to Herman on his first

deployment, and she didn't want to know. But he'd sure hit the nail on the head with his prediction. He sensed his last day coming, and he was dead-nuts accurate.

Did he attract it?

There was another body—Lieutenant John Washington. He was an extremely good looking and likable Afro-American. Of all people. He wasn't even with their battalion. He was just hitching a ride to the landing strip to go home on leave. He had a newborn baby he had never seen. He didn't have to go out with the guys and trace down that stupid wire that led into a booby trap. Of all the rotten luck. Now he was dead, and Chris had another body to bundle and get back to base. It was too dangerous for a chopper. A chopper could be shot down easily.

The 451 didn't have body bags—plenty of MRE's, orange spray paint, and birth control pills, but no fucking body bags! She tried to wrap the bodies in Kevlar blankets and strap them to the hoods of Humvees. There was no one to help her and she struggled with the weight. She had to tie the head and shoulders on first then lift the legs. The bodies kept leaking fluids and sliding off. She gagged and pulled herself together. She had a job to do and she was going to do it.

An Iraqi interpreter who was with the convoy, appeared out of the darkness and tried to help her. She didn't trust the interpreters any further than she could throw them. For all she knew, this interpreter had double crossed them and sold their destination and route to the insurgents. He was still alive wasn't he, without a scratch on him? "Get the fuck away from me." She almost said "Camel Jock," but caught herself.

"Crease, Crease." He called her 'Crease.' "Let me help you. I strong."

"I got it. Go see if there's anymore bodies." She had learned this ploy as a civilian paramedic, especially at car accidents. Give the wannabe helpers something to do. It satisfies their need to help and keeps them out of her hair. "Here, hold this bag and don't move," or "Go help with the gurney."

Gorkin! She forgot about Gorkin! She climbed back inside the Humvee. He was still on the ceiling of the upside down vehicle. He was gasping and choking and waving one hand at her while trying to hold the compress on his neck with the other. He was sputtering frothy, bloody words she couldn't understand.

"Slow down," she said. "What? What?"

"I can't breath," he gasped. Blood was foaming around the edges of his mouth—a bad sign—air was mixing with blood.

"Trach me," he said.

"Trach you? Jesus Christ! Are you fucking out of your mind?" She had only trached people who were unconscious. You can't trach a conscious person.

"For the love of God," she screamed to the ceiling of the Humvee, which was the floor. "Can we get a Medevac?"

She knew the answer.

So there she sat, suctioning Gorkin on the long, bumpy ride, after they got him transferred to another vehicle, back to base camp where he went into surgery.

She still had a gash on her right thigh to attend to, and maybe a broken thumb. She cleaned the gash with Betadine and alcohol, letting herself scream from the pain. The screaming felt good. She then field stitched the wound, without Novocaine, not wanting to pull the doctor away from the seriously wounded, or use up valuable resources. She splinted her thumb, not knowing if it was broken or not.

The other female medics came to meet her. They all knew

about the mission gone bad. It was part of protocol: talk about the incident.

"You doing okay?" they asked.

"No. But I'm working on it. Give me some time."

They gave her space.

Back home in Erkson, Iowa, where Medic Chris Mitchel was from, her husband, Sergeant Jocko Mitchel, of the Erkson Police Department, was busy on patrol. (Jocko was his real name. His mother wanted to call him John, and his father, Jack. They compromised.) Jocko had asked to go back on Patrol from Investigation because there was too much paperwork time with Investigation, making too much time for him to brood and worry about Chris. On patrol he could keep himself busy with domestic disputes, car wrecks and issuing tickets. Chris and he had only been married two months when Chris was deployed. And she was six months away from discharge when she was deployed. For cripes sake.

Jocko had so many mixed feelings. Would she be faithful? He'd heard the stories about women in the military: there were the ones who were looking for men, and the ones who were easy targets for men. Was there an in-between?

It wasn't only Chris. Could he be faithful? There were good looking women right there in his department, some single, some married, who let him know that if he got lonely...well.

One of the nice things about the National Guard was that he had gone to school with some of the members of the 451 and was friends with many of them. There were even a couple of policemen from the department who were on active duty with the 451. He had made an agreement with a couple of his closest friends who were activated, that they would look after Chris, protect her, and give her anything she needed. And it worked in reverse for Chris. She knew soldiers who had spouses in the police department. What went on in Iraq and what went on in Erkson, was easily relayed back and forth.

Also, when Chris had her pre-deployment training at Ft. Sill, Oklahoma, Jocko and a wife of one of the soldiers, Becky, who was a police officer, drove out together to see their spouses. It was a tight knit group.

Jocko was sort of proud of Chris for being in the National Guard, and envious also. She had the opportunity to serve her country. She looked sharp in her uniform, and he was pleased to be married to a person who knew who she was, where she was going, and what the mission was — unlike so many of the scatterbrained wives of policemen he knew.

Jocko had suggested that she go off the pill before deployment, and get pregnant. That would be an automatic out. But Chris wouldn't hear of it. She had an obligation to serve and provide medical aid to the soldiers she had served with, and by golly she was going to do it, no ifs, ands, or buts.

Jocko just prayed she would come back alive. He didn't really understand the 451's job of route clearance and convoy escort. Escort with the police department was pretty easy, and the officers bid for those jobs. It involved driving ahead of parades and funeral processions, and blocking off intersections. Stuff like that.

What the 451 was trained for at Ft. Sill, and what they were actually doing, didn't seem to be related. But maybe that was just the military. The police department could be pretty screwed up at times, too. You just learned to go with the flow. He hated the term, "It is what it is," but if the shoe fits, wear it.

He missed her so much. He had to take her clothes out of their bedroom closet when she was deployed, and put them in the spare bedroom. The clothes smelled like Chris and reminded him of her. He would bury his face in her bathrobe, cry, and want to satisfy himself. It was just easier to remove the reminder, the temptation.

They spent a lot of time on the phone and on the computer communicating back and forth. Because of the time difference, some nights he would look up from the computer, and it would be getting light, and he would have to go to work. Where had the night gone?

He had two horses to care for and he loved to ride and work outdoors. However, the horses were Chris' and they reminded him of her.

So when Jocko got the call from Becky, the woman he rode out to Ft. Sill with, that something had happened that involved Chris (Becky didn't know the details) Jocko was on high alert.

Late that night, on the computer, Chris revealed that there was a major incident that involved her. She was alright, and safe, and he was not to worry. When she got home they would be able to discuss it better. When Jocko pressed for more information, all she said was, "Herman Stein got his Purple Heart."

"What? Huh?" Jocko didn't know who Herman Stein was and what the significance of a "Purple Heart" meant, for sure. It could mean anything from being wounded to wasted. But one thing was for sure, Chris had been involved in some major fighting and trauma.

But, hell, she was a paramedic for the Erkson hospital before she was deployed, so she was no rookie when it came to bloody scenes and violence. The difference, he supposed, was that as a civilian paramedic, she was usually working on strangers—car wrecks, heart attacks, etc. With the 451, she was closely associated with the people she had trained with, and the incidents were usually all trauma.

In his own experience as a police officer, he had seen and been involved with plenty of nasty incidents. He had even shot and killed a person. Jocko had become calloused to the feelings of victims and witnesses to violence. "Deal with it. Move on," he wanted to tell them. He knew from his training that the average person was involved with two, maybe three major trauma events in their lifetime. For police officers, over their careers, it was 800. It was easy to become calloused.

Where Chris fit into all that spectrum, he wasn't sure. Could a major traumatic incident eat her lunch, or could she deal with it? He knew from his own experience that people often said they were alright, when, in reality, they were dying inside. He wished he could be there to support her.

Then when he was moving her stuff out of the bedroom, he ran across a letter in some personal items she had sent back from Ft. Sill. It was a love letter to a "Bob," saying how much she wanted to be with him and missed him and would make it up to him when they were finally together.

Jocko froze. A sick feeling swept through him like he had never felt before. The military handed out free birth control pills to the female medics that they took year round so they wouldn't menstruate on mission. Ugly thoughts racked his brain.

Fortunately, and by the Grace of God, Chris was able to detect that something was wrong that night on their computer communication. She made him spit it out.

"Okay, I found a love letter in your things that you wrote to 'Bob.' Have you been..."

Chris burst out laughing. "That was a letter I wrote for silly Priscilla who was having boyfriend problems and needed help writing a letter. She's dumb as a rock. They got things patched up and I forgot about the letter. You're my man, Jocko. There is no other. When I come home, we're gonna have a family."

Jocko picked up on the word "when." It wasn't "if." He had no doubt that she would be home, she was faithful, and they were meant to be.

Mission Accomplished

Scot Victor watched the medic work on the little Iraqi girl. She was still alive, although hurt badly. She just stared up at the Medic — big brown eyes, half afraid of the infidel female without burka — half trusting, mostly scared. Scot looked over to where the Medevac Helicopter was being loaded with three dead marines. "Why?" he asked himself. The Marines were dead. The little girl wasn't. She should go. They could save her.

The little girl died later on the ground.

It was one of those times Scot told himself he was a soldier, not a civilian, and to push on with the mission. Things happened in war, in the military, he had no business questioning.

It was a vehicle-born IED. The soldiers called them "V-BIEDS"--suicide bombers coming at them in a vehicle, some wearing the explosives like a vest, others with a trunk full. The gunner on top of the Humvee was supposed to waste them before they got close. But the rusty Datsun pick-up came out of nowhere, fast, partially covered with tattered camouflage. The gunner on top of the Humvee was looking the other direction. When he saw the V-BIED, it was too late.

Scot was in an APC (Armored Personnel Carrier). The blast knocked him unconscious. When he came to, on the floor, his ears ringing, he grabbed his weapon and went for the hatch. Another soldier pulled him down, shaking his head. Scot didn't have to ask why. Later Scot would realize the soldier, he didn't even know his name, maybe saved his life.

It was Scot's birthday. He was 19.

He had been Homecoming King his senior year. It surprised him. He didn't think he was that popular. It was mostly because of his brother, two years older than Scot. His brother had been a jock-stud, Grover's "Mr. Football."

Coming back from boot camp between his junior and senior year, Scot had lost his baby fat and was in the best shape of his life. But he hadn't been able to attend summer football camp like the rest of the guys. Coach Kuntz, seeing the new Scot, switched him from defensive tackle to offensive fullback. He hadn't had time to digest the play book. The offensive plays were complicated. "Kick ass is all you have to do, like your brother," the coach told him.

They were on the three yard line. Coach Kuntz sent in the play. Instead of calling the play by name, which the coach knew Scot might not understand, he simply said, "Give the ball to Scot." Scot scored his one and only touchdown, and got to stand with the pretty homecoming queen at halftime. She wouldn't look him in the eye, and wasn't sure of his name.

This morning, on their mission of convoy escort, Scot had seen three dead men, hooded and hanging from a bridge. The smell was horrible, unlike anything he'd ever smelled. Worse than the burning trash in the dump they'd just passed. The men had been shot, from what Scot could tell. It made him sick. The insurgents would kill anyone they thought was giving intel to the Americans or helping the Americans in any way. It didn't make any difference if the locals had families or not. Just round'm up and kill'm.

At least these locals had been shot, and not beheaded like Scot had seen before — the ones the insurgents really wanted to make an example of—interpreters, or suspected interpreters. Scot's platoon had to leave the bodies where they were. It was another one of those times he had to tell himself he was a soldier, not a civilian. Stay on mission.

The recruiter had come to his home when Scot was 17. "We're the National Guard, not the Army. We stay in nation, help out in floods, natural disasters, things like that. We'll pay for his college education."

You betcha.

Scot had been getting his physical at Camp Green. It was 4:30 in the morning and they were having breakfast. Scot was thinking, "I can't eat this early." CNN was on the television. There was a reporter in a Jeep bouncing across the desert in Iraq. The invasion had started. The other guys at the table were cheering, "We'll see some action!"

Scot was thinking. "What the fuck? What did I get myself into?"

They flew to Iraq on New Year's Eve. It was dark in the airplane and there was no heat or air conditioning. They were either hot or cold. "If I was home," Scot was thinking, "I'd be drinking with the guys. Party time USA. Get'n laid."

It was so noisy in the C-47 that the roar seemed like it was coming from inside of his head, resonating from his skull. "You know why they're flying us on New Year's Eve, don't cha?" the kid beside him screamed.

Scot shook his head.

"This way we'll land in Iraq on New Year's Day. Iraq is a War Zone. They won't have to pay us combat pay for December."

Scot let this soak into his head. It was the first time he thought of the military as adversarial.

But he didn't have time to think about it long. The transport plane they were in dropped straight down 20,000 feet like it had hit an air pocket. If they hadn't been strapped in they would have been pinned to the ceiling. The plane then did a hard right and went into a nose-first spiral. The soldier beside him threw up, vomit flying to the ceiling. Someone screamed. Scot thought they'd been hit by enemy fire. Then the plane hit the ground like a 100-ton sack of potatoes and the lights came on. A voice over the intercom stuttered, "Sorry 'bout that, boys and girls. Not really. It's what we gotta do to not draw enemy fire. Hope your lunch set awright."

Scot could hardly move. His legs felt like rubber and he had a splitting headache from the rapid change in altitude. But he was on the ground and about to get his first taste of Iraq. Literally.

The heat was unbelievable, like a hot, dry oven, one that had some burnt food in it. He would come to associate that heat and smell and taste with war, and in the middle of the night, even years later, that smell and taste would come back to him in dreams, and he thought he was still in Iraq.

His first few months in Iraq were spent stringing communication wires between palm trees. "This is not what I trained for," he said to himself, and to anyone who would listen. But everyone was in the same boat as him. He had been trained to kick in doors and take prisoners and keep his head down. Instead he was dangled by the back of his trousers, high in the air by a cherry picker, so he could string wire, a sitting or hanging duck for a sniper. He felt vulnerable and exposed, which he was for sure, but once again, he was a soldier and followed orders.

He wasn't trained for route clearance or convoy escort either. But that's what Charlie Company was assigned to do. Combat Engineers were supposed to build bridges and blow shit up.

Instead, they looked for IED's so the convoy wouldn't get blown to bits — the convoy, not them.

There was a constant dry taste in his mouth, that was part sand and part fear. "Let's see," he asked himself. "Just why in the hell did I join the Guard? Oh, yeah, so it would pay for my college education and I could help people. Help people my ass." He looked around at the general population. They didn't want soldiers there. They hated the U.S. It was even scrawled on some of the stone walls, "Go home, Ankee."

Scot wanted to go home. What had he been thinking?

At least he knew some of the soldiers he served with, which helped. He had gone to school with some of them, knew their families and their stories. They had stories a lot like his. There was a mixture of gung-ho and fear and just plain give-a-shit in every one of them. The fear he noticed had a certain odor. It was in their sweat, which they did a lot of in this 110 to 120 degree heat and added to the bad taste in his mouth. It tasted like what he thought burnt cardboard might taste like.

Scot was appalled at the Humvees they were driving. There was cloth for doors, and the floors were made of thin tin. They lined the floors with sand bags and mechanics cut out half-inch steel plate to "up armor" the vehicles. But it added weight, lots of weight, that the vehicles weren't designed to carry. "See that Humvee, there, Victor?" one of his buddies said, nudging him in the ribs. The Humvee looked squat and was listing to one side, like it had midriff bulge. "It's riding on the frame. The driver has very little control over its steering. This is the 'Go-to-war-with-the-Army-we-have' bullshit. This is suicide. We might as well surrender."

Scot tried to block out negativity. But it was a struggle.

Especially when the rockets came in every day. The area they lived in around Ramadi was called "Rocket Alley." It was hard getting used to, not knowing whether today was the day you were going to get it, and you wouldn't be going home, except in a box. But he did get used to it. He could tell by the sound of the rockets whether they were close or not. He even went jogging.

One day when he went for a run, around midday, he heard the whine and whoosh of a rocket overhead, but knew it wasn't close, so he just continued with his run. The rocket hit on the other side of a berm, several hundred meters to his left. He didn't think too much of it.

The next day he heard two Marines were killed by that rocket. It was a stop-in-his-tracks moment. Two people he didn't even know lost their lives. How could that be? How should he feel? He was getting calloused. Some people made it home, others didn't. Cannon fodder.

On a cache sweep, Scot's metal detector indicated something was just below the surface of the sand. He went digging, careful and mindful about the possibility of it being a trap, wired for detonation. Scot and his buddies found a freezer full of munitions and bomb making supplies. But what made the hair on the back of his neck stand up was there was a chopped off hand on top of the pile of munitions. What message the bomb maker was trying to send and to whom was a mystery. Was it meant for the U.S. Military? Fuck with us and you're gonna die, Mother Fucker. Or was it meant for the general population? Betray us and this is what you're gonna get. Scot remembered the story in the Bible where the punishment for stealing was chopping off a hand.

It was a chilling moment for Scot. He would see that hand in his dreams for years after his deployment. Sometimes the hand moved. Once it even raised its middle finger to him. At other times the hand was rotted black and smelled. Scot often had sense of smell and hearing in his dreams, and saw colors that changed from black and white to color, especially red. Lots of red.

However, it was the sound of snarling and gnashing teeth that really bothered him, like he was dying and going to Hell.

Sometimes the guys (and gals) in Charlie Company, even Scott, could be mean to civilians. They had one local riding with them they taught to say "Fuck You" in broken English. They would ride through the streets and the local would say "Fock Eue" to everyone they passed. It was hilarious and sad at the same time. They had a civilian who was voicing what they all felt. At the end of the day, Scot knew it wasn't right, but it was still just one of those deals. Soldiers can be crude in a foreign land, far from home, very crude. Animals really.

But there was worse yet. MRE's (Meals Ready to Eat) came in sealed plastic bags. The soldiers would take these into the field on a mission, eat their meals, then some would save the bags to defecate in. It was great sport to throw the bags at civilians as they passed by. It was no wonder the general population hated the U.S. Military.

Counter that with some of the goodwill programs the 451 engaged in, like getting school supplies to needy children, building schools, and setting up voting stations. The general population was confused and had mixed feelings about the U.S. The U.S. was bipolar: on the rampage one moment, kind and gentle the next, saying, "Trust us."

Who are we? Scot wondered. Friend or foe?

Scot was plagued with the question of why they were there.

He was too young to remember what the U.S. went through with Vietnam. It was the same question then, he heard: "Why were we there?" There were riots in the streets over that question and Vietnam Vets were treated like shit. Now, the U.S. had been attacked, so the perpetrators had to be tracked down and punished. But was the U.S. really doing that here in Iraq, or just trying to protect U.S. soldiers from being killed? The perpetrators or would be perpetrators just fled to another country.

Was it oil? Or was the U.S. nation building—trying to convert a country into a Democracy, a country ten times the age of the United States? Maybe it was the U.S. that should learn from Iraq.

These were questions that constantly bugged Scot, questions that soldiers shouldn't be asking, questions that stood in the way of him performing his job to his utmost ability.

Toward the end of his deployment, Scot was given the cushy job of driving the Colonel around. On one of his last days incountry, Scot picked the Colonel up after a meeting. The Colonel had a smirk on his face. Scot asked, "Why the smile, Colonel? Get a little from Rosie last night?"

"Just drive, Victor."

A few miles later, Scot, noticing the smile still there, not characteristic of the Colonel, who could be an asshole at times (most of the time), asked again, "Why so happy?"

"Okay, Victor, if you insist. There are three other battalions in Iraq that do about the same thing we do. The other three battalions combined didn't pick up and destroy as many IED's as we did. I'm damn proud of that. Mission accomplished. Dingman and Jones with their computers and statistics and probability really know their shit."

Scot thought a lot about that on the plane ride home. Mission accomplished. Was the war in the Middle East any closer to being over because that mission was accomplished? Was Iraq any better off? Was the United States any better off?

He had his doubts.

Colonel Bert Price

The only reason 17-year old Bert Price signed up for the Army Reserves was because he felt his dad was against it. Not that Bert was that rebellious as a youth, it was more like the military was not a part of his family so he thought, "What the hell?" And it was a way to pay college expenses. He was a junior at Central High School in Grover. He met the recruiter and was impressed. Bert thought, "I'd like to try this."

As a sophomore at the University of Northern Iowa, he signed up for ROTC. The Company Commander was the wrestling coach at Erkson High School and an awesome dude, in Bert's estimation. The CC said, "You'll be an officer, a lieutenant, what a great opportunity." Bert liked opportunities.

He was an English major at UNI, sort of by quirk. There was a TA, a first year female, who had the audacity to slap an F on one of Bert's papers. Bert had been rather pleased with his writing. When he inquired about the F, she said, "You had no plan. You just sat down and wrote random thoughts."

She was right. He needed to have a plan, and then to execute the plan. English was as good a curriculum as any.

Some of the guys ribbed him. "English and ROTC? That's sort of quirky, an oxymoron, ain't it?"

Bert didn't know what "oxymoron" meant so he looked it up. They were right. English Literature, writing and the military seemed at odds, but Bert liked that. Maybe English would be good for the military, and the military good for English. "A plan," he said to his roommate. "That's what I need, a plan. Man with a plan."

"Huh?" said the roommate.

After graduating, Bert tried teaching with his BA in English. His father was a teacher, as well as his brother and sister. Teaching was honorable. But all he could land was a special education, substitute teaching position at Cedar Falls High School. They were kids with disciplinary issues, whom mainstream teachers didn't want anymore. Bert was 22. One of his students was 20 and bigger than he was.

"Teaching might not be for me," he thought. "Not without a masters degree."

Young Price was drilling the whole time with the National Guard and not really enjoying it. He had completed his officer training course and wanted to be a platoon leader. He asked around and found out the 451st Engineering Battalion in NE Iowa had an opening for a platoon leader. The 451st was Erkson, Grover and all of NE Iowa. He joined the 451st in the summer of 1990 and got married.

In January he and his wife, Margaret, moved into an apartment. She was pregnant when Bert got the notice that the 451 was going to mobilize for deployment to Germany and Kuwait. "What the hell?" he said.

Margaret squinted her eyes.

The 451 was going to move in for mop-up operations following General Norman Schwarzkopf's invasion of Kuwait. Schwarzkopf was to drive out the forces of Saddam Hussein in Operation Desert Storm. Except Storm'n Norman kicked the shit out of Saddam Hussein's forces, and the 451st was left sitting on the tarmac in Germany, where they trained and trained and trained. Which was beneficial to young Lieutenant Price. He learned the military inside and out, and liked what he learned.

Lieutenant Price also met Sergeant Dwight Jones. Dwight was the NBC (Nuclear Biological Chemical) NCO for the 451st, and was a "My way or the highway" type of E5. Price was a little taken aback by what he determined to be Jones' near insolence, but it was a good experience for Price to meet such a squared away, determined, and knowledgeable enlisted man. He put his trust in Dwight right away. With the Weapons of Mass Destruction that Saddam was known to have stockpiled somewhere, Jones' expertise would be invaluable.

Both Price and Jones were disappointed that the 451st was shipped home instead of participating in the invasion, but as Dwight said, "The word 'war' ain't in the middle of Schwarzkopf's name, for nothing, Lieutenant. Storm'n Norman is the soldier's soldier."

Bert's first son was born while they were deployed.

When they returned, Bert started working on his Master's Degree in English at UNI. It would take him seven years to complete (he took one course per semester), and he thought he would never get finished, but he did. He contemplated a PhD, but at the pace it took him to get his Master's, a Doctorate would take 20. Bert put the kibosh on a PhD right away.

He had made Lt. Colonel anyway. That was as good or better than any PhD.

Arnold Allen Schwarzendruber, Rules of Engagement

Colonel Price usually didn't go out with a platoon on a route clearance mission. He had too many other priorities, and it was too dangerous. But he wanted to go on this one. It was going to be conducted in the middle of the day, rather than night as usual, to convey a specific message to the Iraqis: "You can trust us. We want you to come forward with information that will help you live a better life." A message of this nature was not possible if the route-clearance team was operating at night—the night being too full of darkness.

He checked his watch for the date. It was April 11, 2007. As always, the 11th day of the month still carried with it that feeling of catastrophe. The terrorists had struck the United States on September 11th, and started this whole mess the US was still embroiled in.

The 451 was going into the worst part of Ramadi, where there were the most IED's per square kilometer, where more U.S. soldiers had been killed than in any other part of Iraq, and where the Iraqis lived in abject squalor. There was trash and garbage everywhere, even human sewage in the streets. Part of 451's mission, besides clearing IED's, and gaining information about the enemy, was to clean up the streets. They hauled truck load after truck load of garbage and trash out and burned it in the desert.

The 451 had toys for the kids. It was tricky business. The kids wanted the toys desperately, but they knew if they were seen taking gifts from the American soldiers their families could be targeted by the insurgents, or the kids could receive whippings from their parents. But a few of them still couldn't resist the gifts of toys and candy.

The heat was stifling. Price could hardly breathe and his blouse was already soaked with sweat, and sticking to his skin. He wanted to take the blouse off but knew regulations: fully covered at all times. He had to set the example for his men.

Colonel Price was busy handing out gifts to a small group of children, when he noticed that the city was quiet. Strange. Ramadi is a very large city, and it was the middle of the day — a time when there was usually a lot of noise and activity, cars honking and vendors hawking their wares. But everything was quiet. He keyed the mic. "What's going on?"

"Uh, we have an IED here, Colonel. We're going to go ahead and secure it."

"Okay, I'll make sure you have plenty of cover."

There was one crack.

Price knew immediately it was a rifle shot. But there was no other.

Then came the words he didn't want to hear. "Man down."

"Fuck!" Price said to his driver.

The driver wrinkled his eyebrows.

Price pointed to the other end of the convoy. "Get me down there. Quick," he ordered the driver.

"There's no way, sir. I can't get around the convoy."

"Up on the walk."

"But, sir!"

"Go, now!"

The driver did what he was ordered and drove up on the sidewalk, hanging meat and goods flying everywhere." Iraqis scrambled out of the way like bowling pins. All the goodwill the 451 had worked for that morning was destroyed.

They came upon a body lying in the street. It was Spec 5 Arnold Schwarzendruber. He had a hole through his throat about the size of his little finger. His eyes were wide open and he had a surprised look on his face. Everybody called him Arnold Schwarzenegger. Like Arnie Schwarzenegger, he was a big man, well over six feet tall, and solidly built.

"I told him to get his head down," the First Sergeant said.

The gunner on the Humvee hollered, "It had to've come from that tower right there on that mosque. Want me to waste it, Colonel?"

"Did you see the shot come from there, Corporal Howard?"

"Naw, Sir."

"Then stand down." Colonel Price hated Rules of Engagement. The U.S. Military had them, the enemy didn't. Return fire only when fired at, and you know where it's coming from.

"I'm calling in Medevac," barked the First Sergeant.

"Medevac?" Price was incredulous. "This soldier is dead. Medevac is going to do him no good. Besides, there's no place to set a Black Hawk down, with all the wires."

"I'm calling in Medevac." The First Sergeant was surprisingly surly, and it irritated Price. "We can use that soccer field to the south."

"That is a complete waste of resources, Sergeant."

The sergeant stepped real close to Colonel Price's face and whispered. Price could smell Key chewing tobacco on his breath. All the soldiers chewed, instead of smoked. Cigarette smoke drew enemy fire. "The men at the other end of the convoy don't know he's dead, Colonel. All they know is a soldier's been shot. I have promised that if any of them get hurt, they will get the best medical care in the world."

"Gotcha, Sergeant. Call in Medevac. Go for it. What the hell?"

Colonel Price reached down and touched the toe of Arnold

Allen Schwarzendruber's boot and said a little prayer. "Even though I walk through the valley of the shadow of death, I shall fear no evil, for Thou art with me. Thy rod and Thy staff they comfort me." Price knew that Arnold Allen Schwarzendruber was one of three soldiers in the 451 that had listed Atheist for religion on their dog tags. He hoped that Schwarzendruber could hear him from wherever he was and know that his soul was being prayed for.

Stale Cigarette

Chaplain Joe Fordice stared at the universal symbol of a fallen soldier: the soldier's weapon, in this instance an M-16, the bayonet end stuck in the ground, the soldier's helmet on the stock, and his dog tags dangling from the rifle. Also, as tradition would have it, the other members of the fallen soldier's platoon brought personal items of the soldier's, or something they wanted to remember him by, and laid them on the ground around the weapon.

Chaplain Fordice continued to stare at the items, unable to move, unable to perform his job. There was an ammunition belt, boots, jack knife, nail clippers, a tattered picture of the soldier's family, and other items belonging to fallen soldier, Sergeant Arnold Allen Schwarzendruber. It was the Chaplain's job, after the service, to round up the items and send them to the fallen soldier's family.

One item caught the chaplain's eye. It was a single, unfiltered cigarette stuck haphazardly in the trigger guard of the M-16, a Pall Mall. Arnold Allen Schwarzendruber had been a heavy smoker, although he chewed instead of smoked when he was on mission. All the soldiers knew tobacco smoke, or the glow of a cigarette, could attract the eyes of a sniper. It was when he was off duty, back in his hutch, that Arnold Allen Schwarzendruber "smoked like a chimney." Ironically, he had a wad of Red Man stuck in his cheek when the sniper's bullet went through his throat.

Chaplain Fordice almost gagged when he thought about it. He had tried to chew once, maybe twice, and gotten sick to his stomach. It also left a bad taste in his mouth. But the men told him the buzz they got from chew was better and longer lasting than smoked tobacco. "Maybe so," Chaplain Fordice said out loud to no one. "Maybe it was that chaw that attracted that 5.6 millimeter sniper round, that made that neat little hole through Arnie's Adam's Apple, and put that permanent surprised look on his face." Chaplain Fordice had a vision of tobacco juice spewing out of the bullet hole.

Chaplain Fordice wiped his forearm across his eyes trying to clear his thoughts. He was too confused. There were too many people dying. "For what reason?" he whispered, his throat dry and parched from the blistering heat, and the omnipresent sand—sand that got in his teeth, eyes, nose, food, canteen, bed, clothes, everything.

"Why are we here?" he whispered again. "What is our purpose? We know the mission. The mission is simple: find and remove IED's. But what is the purpose? These people don't want us here. Why are we here? Because some hijackers took down the Twin Towers?" He looked around as if someone was going to answer these questions for him. There was no one.

To add to the confusion, Arnold Schwarzendruber was an atheist. And here they had been conducting a funeral service for him, after a fashion. The religious part had been left out, but Colonel Price had still wanted the chaplain to conduct a service for the platoon. After all, that's what a funeral service is for—the living, not the dead. So Chaplain Fordice didn't read Scripture, he didn't say, "I am the way, and the truth, and the life: no one cometh unto the Father, but by me," like he would normally recite at a "believers" funeral. Instead he talked in generalities—what is our mission? We don't always know. We are to follow orders and look out for each other. "Arnold Allen Schwarzendruber believed in what he was doing and that country and service came first. We are here to honor him."

"God dammit!" Chaplain Fordice shouted out loud and dropped to his knees, his hands outstretched and palms upturned. He was looking at the sky, looking for God, for an answer. "What are we doing here? Please tell me!"

He missed his wife and kids terribly. His kids were having birthdays and he wasn't there. He was missing their growing up, teaching them how to ride a bike, fish, play catch. They needed him. He needed them.

He looked down at Arnold Schwarzendruber's personal items and began picking them up, one by one, studying each one, looking for Arnold Schwarzendruber in each, then putting the items in a backpack to hide them from the light of day, to erase the memory of Arnold Allen Schwarzendruber, as if by shutting those keepsakes away, he could erase the soldier. Chaplain Fordice would send these belongings to Schwarzendruber's family so they could cry and reminisce and ask, "Why?" Dog tags and medals were always prized, frameable possessions of a soldier who was killed in battle. Although Arnold Schwarzendruber wasn't really killed in battle. Action yes, but not battle. He was on a mission, a mission that more than irritated the local Iraqis, but a mission nonetheless. He had his head stuck up too high, and had been told to pull his head in, but ignored the warning so that he could look around. Look at the decadence, the marketplace, hanging meat—goat, chicken, rats, whatever. The sewer filled streets, the half naked kids running around, almost getting run over by tank tracks, begging candy from the troops, and offering their sisters, "She virgin. Five dolla."

Chaplain Fordice looked again at the old cigarette stuck between the trigger and trigger guard. It was nearly broke in half, but still intact. Chaplin Fordice couldn't send a cigarette home to Arnold Schwarzendruber's family. What would they think? Someone had put the cigarette there more in remembrance of

Arnold Schwarzendruber smoking non-stop, lighting one cigarette off of the other—sometimes holding one in each hand—when he got back to his hutch after a mission. He was even known to chew and smoke at the same time—really gone-to-hell tobacco use. Why? Did it help block out the home sickness? Chaplain Fordice wondered—the fear, the anger, the guilt.

Always the guilt, omnipresent like the sand, only stuck in his craw, in his chest.

Chaplain Fordice pulled the cigarette out of the trigger guard. Dried tobacco spilled from the end. He licked and twisted the end of the cigarette shut so the tobacco wouldn't spill out, like a joint, he thought, and stuck it in his blouse pocket. In his college days he had smoked marijuana some, like most everyone else. "Don't Bogart that joint," he remembered was the saying. "How naive we were," he thought. "We thought we would save the world. We didn't save shit."

Later that night, he walked out into the desert. Camp Ramadi was so big, he could walk out into wide open space and still be within the confines of The Wire. It was so dark. There was no light pollution. The sky was pure black with crystal sharp stars and planets—Venus, or was it Jupiter? He wished he knew his planets and constellations better. Was that Orion? The Big Dipper was obvious, but others he wasn't sure of. He had never seen night sky like this before, and wondered if this was the same sky, the same stars that led the shepherds, the Wise Men to the baby Jesus, bearing gifts. Gifts for what? A fucked up world?

The soldiers sometimes came to him to confide that they couldn't do their job anymore, that they were sick of "playing soldier," that they wanted to go home, be with their family, lead a "normal life."

What is normal? the chaplain wondered. What could he say

to these young men? Some of them were barely 18 — kids really, seeing their buddies blown to bits by IED's, innocent children and civilians as "collateral damage." What could the chaplain tell these soldiers? "You must do your job, you can't go home. Just six more months. You can make it. I will pray for you."

"Don't waste your breath, Chaplain. There ain't no God. Would a loving God allow this?"

What could he say?

Then one time a soldier's sergeant came to him and asked what the soldier had confided.

"I can't tell you that, Sergeant. You know what's shared between a pastor and his fold is confidential."

"Tell me, Goddammit," the sergeant said. "I need to know so I will know how to soldier him. It's for the good of the platoon."

"No. I won't tell you."

The sergeant was real pissed, but Chaplain Fordice stuck to his guns.

"Stuck to his guns. Ha! What a term," he said to himself. (Chaplains didn't carry weapons.) "Like the cigarette in the trigger guard, now nearly broken in half — like the man."

He fumbled in his shirt pocket for the cigarette. He hadn't smoked in years. What was he doing? He had planned this because he had brought a Bic lighter borrowed from one of the soldiers. "What do you need a lighter for, preacher? You haven't gone wonky on us, have you?"

Maybe he was wonky. Did he dare light this cigarette and maybe draw the eyes of a sniper somewhere out there? To hell with it! A quick shot through the throat like Arnold Schwarzendruber, and it would all be over real fast. A welcome end maybe.

He thought about Arnold Schwarzendruber. The soldiers all

called him Arnie Schwarzenegger. And in a lot of ways, he was like Arnie Schwarzenegger — big, tall, slow talking, patriotic, intentional movements — like every word, every action was meant to instill pride, toughness. "I'll be bock," he was fond of saying.

But he didn't come bock.

The real Arnold Schwarzenegger had never been a soldier. It had all been an act. A spoof. To get young men killed.

Where do atheists go? Chaplain Fordice wondered. Is there a holding place for atheists, a Purgatory, a Limbo? Are atheists' souls eternal, like he believed Christian souls were? What about Muslims? They believed their souls were eternal, too. Did Christian souls and Muslim souls meet up somewhere and unite, become one? Friends even? The lion will lay down with the lamb.

Too many thoughts. Too much chatter in his head. If he could stop the chatter he could be at peace. He lit the cigarette, inhaled deeply and nearly threw up. A gush of saliva filled his mouth and throat, and a sick feeling gripped his stomach. He took another deep inhalation and this time did throw up, a burning, smelly, bile.

Then the high hit him. He could feel it crawling up his spine to the back of his neck and into his brain, spreading like a river on parched land. His hair tingled, the skin on his scalp tightened. He thought the top of his head was going to come off.

And those were the only feelings he had: sick to his stomach, high as a kite, a bad taste in his mouth, but the absence of chatter. There was just a wild, crazy buzzing. But the chatter was gone.

Guard Duty

Colonel Price had a disciplinary allegation to handle, although there wasn't much "allegation" about it. There was a video of the whole incident that didn't leave anything to the imagination.

There were guard towers on the perimeter of Camp Ramadi that had to be manned 24/7. Guard duty could be pretty boring, as 99.9% of the time there was nothing happening.

To alleviate the boredom, Corporal Ransom had invited Spec 5 Sweeny, a female medic, up for a little "tryst," while he was on guard duty. He video recorded the whole encounter on a camcorder. Sweeny knew they were being video recorded and didn't care.

Corporal Ransom had borrowed the camcorder from a buddy, and when he returned it, he told his buddy, "Hey, I left a little something on it for you."

There was a little something alright—the whole scene in graphic detail. The buddy got a charge out of it and showed it to all his friends.

Word got around pretty fast, and it was soon brought to the attention of Colonel Price. Fraternization in the military, more bluntly, sex between soldiers was against regulations.

Price saw the female medic, Sweeny, first. When she showed no remorse, and seemed to think it was funny, Price busted her two ranks, and had her shipped back to the states. He couldn't have her being a target for every lonely/horny soldier in the battalion. Her main response was, "They give us these birth control pills so we won't have periods, what do you expect?"

If she hadn't said that, Price might have been a little more lenient.

As Specialist Sweeny walked away, Colonel Prices couldn't help but notice her figure. She was quite shapely. Damn he was homesick for his wife and family.

It was Corporal Ransom that really pissed him off. Ransom seemed proud of his "conquest," and said as much, and that he would do it again, given the boredom of guard duty.

"So, what you're telling me, Corporal Ransom, is that you put Camp Ramadi in jeopardy for a piece of ass. Insurgents do occasionally test our perimeter you know,"

"C'mon, Colonel," Corporal Ransom laughed, "I could still see out the window when she was blowing me."

That did it. Price busted Ransom to an E1, suspended his pay for a month, and limited his rations.

"Tell me, Private Ransom," Price asked before he left, "why did you think that video wouldn't get you in trouble?"

"Really?" Private Ransom started to get some seriousness to him. "Compared to some of the other videos floating around Ramadi, this is tame stuff, Colonel."

Price thought about that remark a lot. If anyone should know better, it was him. He had an undergraduate and graduate degree in English from the University of Northern Iowa. He had read Shakespeare, the Greek and Roman Classics, as well as modern authors, like Fitzgerald, Hemingway and D.H. Lawrence. He was well aware of what went on, even several thousand years ago. Why should this incident surprise and shock him? For one thing, both Ransom and Sweeny had spouses back home.

It was just that somehow, he might be naive, but Colonel Price thought the 451, being such an elite group of soldiers, was above all this.

KIA, The Case of Private Volger

Colonel Price stared at his desk. He had a ton of work to do. Command was wanting the 451 to provide transportation support and protection for something called a NERF. Price wasn't even sure what the NERF was. It was a huge piece of equipment on two buffalo chassis that would move across the desert and send out signals that would supposedly detonate IED's ahead of itself. It was great in theory, but Price had heard through the military grapevine that, yes, the NERF would detonate IED's ahead of itself, but it was also blowing up televisions and radios in the homes of Iraqis. "Great," thought Price. "Here we have a dirt poor Iraqi family, and the only piece of technology they have, this portable television, and it gets blown up by American troops. Wonderful." He didn't even know what NERF stood for. It was something like, "Neutralizing Energy Radar Frequency." Maybe. He wasn't sure. All he knew was it was a giant pain in the ass. The 451 was supposed to move it across the desert and provide protection. "Not good. They would be sitting ducks for every insurgent wanting to make a name for himself." He didn't like putting his soldiers at risk for some quack idea like a NERF.

He looked up. There was a soldier standing in front of him. His name tag said, "Volger."

Oh, yeah. He remembered now. Lieutenant Dobbs had sent one of his men in for discipline. Something about Volger refusing to go on mission.

Price looked the young man up and down. He was tall and lanky, hardly 18 by his looks, barely shaving. It was hard to tell. Price looked for the soldier's file somewhere in the "To-do" stack. He found it and glanced at the soldier's age. 25. How could that be?

"So," Colonel Price said. "You don't want to go on mission?"

"I'm done, sir."

"What do you mean, done?"

"I'm not going back out there. I wanna go home to Mamma."

"You know you're talking court martial."

"Yes, sir. Lock me up. At least I'd be safe. Give me a Dishonorable. I'm not going back out there."

Colonel Price dismissed Volger and called in Dobbs. "Give him a day off. Maybe two. Some rest might help."

It was a bad deal. All the soldiers were over worked and here Volger was refusing to go out on mission. After two days Dobbs had him marched to a Humvee and stuffed in.

Three hours into the mission, in 113° brutally dry heat, Volger was handed a bottle of water.

"I'm not drinking," he said.

"What do you mean, you're not drinking?"

"I'm not drinking," he said.

Dobbs called Price. "Pacifist Volger won't drink."

"What do you mean he won't drink?"

"Just what I said. He won't drink. I think he's trying to off himself by dehydration."

Colonel Price couldn't believe what he was hearing. There had been incidents in other battalions of soldiers shooting themselves, some of them successful, but suicide by dehydration? "You tell that fucker he's gonna drink! If he won't, you pour it down his Goddamn throat. Do you understand?"

Dobbs was hesitant. "Uh."

"Uh, what, Dobbs?"

"Private Volger said God will give him manna in heaven. He's delirious. I don't think he's drank water in two days."

"Oh, Jesus Christ. You just get him back here alive. I'll ship his ass out. He's bad for morale."

It didn't take long. It was during the heat of the next day. Volger had convulsions during the night. The other soldiers tried forcing him to drink, but he spat the water out. He turned white, soiled himself and died at 1400 the next day on the return journey to camp.

Colonel Price and Lieutenant Dobbs conferred. Price wanted to know how he was supposed to list Volger's death. "I cannot," he told Dobbs, "tell his parents that their son killed himself by voluntary dehydration."

"Just put down killed in action," Dobbs told him. "Lost in the desert and died."

"And he'll get a Purple Heart."

"It could be worse."

"How's that?"

"At least we're not citing him for valor."

"You're right. KIA."

Blowup

Colonel Price watched the convoy getting ready to go out. It was a four-day mission to the border to get supplies, exchange equipment and pick up mail. The soldiers looked sharp—all had their Kevlar on, helmets, goggles, gloves, ear protectors. The camo cloth of the blouse was UV and Chemical rated, making it even hotter. In the searing temperatures of the desert, it was hard to enforce the dress requirement—no skin unprotected—but it was for their own protection. Sun burns, or more precisely, "sun poisoning" could be so severe it could knock out a company for days, something Price couldn't afford. There were missions that had to deploy, no ifs, ands or buts. He had seen sunburns so bad—skin covered with boils—second degree burns really, that the skin became infected and totally put the soldier out of commission. They had to go on antibiotics. These were Iowa soldiers, men and women who had grown up baling hay, detassling corn, lifeguarding. They were proud of their deep tans—a badge of courage. Here in Iraq? A no go. Price wanted to see lily white skin under that blouse or on the forehead. Farmer tans.

The convoy went out and Colonel Price returned to his desk work. He wished he could go with them, and see some action. The military could "meeting" you to death, and he had a big one coming up. A full accounting with the General. Number of IED's encountered, removed, or detonated. Injuries. Casualities—hopefully none. Challenge coins awarded. Citations. Discipline.

He heard a rumbling. "What the hell?" He looked out the

window and the convoy was coming back. They hadn't been gone an hour. Then he saw something he did not want to see. A soldier sitting out of an open hatch with his blouse off. Price wanted to explode, but checked himself. He knew what the problem was, and it wasn't the soldier. It was their leadership. Poor leadership allows misconduct.

He met with the company commander and found out why they returned. They had been hit with an IED right off the bat. No one was hurt, but one of the units had sprung a fuel leak and they thought it best to return to Ramadi for repairs.

"And the blouse off?" he asked.

The soldier with his blouse off heard the remark and blew up. "Jesus fucking Christ, Colonel. It's a hundred-and-twenty-fucking degrees out here. You expect us to wear this shit?"

"Stand down, Martin," the company commander told him. "You're outta line."

"Fuck him! Who in the hell does he think he is? God? He sits behind his fucking desk all day, in his air-conditioned office, and then rips us for having our blouse off! He can suck my dick!"

Martin had his M4 in one hand and was waving it around.

Colonel Price wondered if he was going to be shot, or if he would have to defend himself. But he wanted to see how far this soldier would carry it and how far the company commander would let it to go. He knew how tempers could flare in the heat and battlefield conditions. Soldiers lives were at stake and here he was quibbling over a blouse off.

As it turned out, the other soldiers, not the company commander, got between Martin and Colonel Price. "Hey, dude, are you fucking crazy? This here's the Colonel. Show a little respect."

"Fuck him and the horse he rode in on!"

Colonel Price let it go until the next day. He had Martin standing at attention in front of him. Martin was a completely different soldier. He hung his head, and wouldn't look the Colonel in the eye.

Price sort of liked the kid. He reminded him of himself when he was that age—defiant, hating authority, wanting to cut his own path, not wanting to take crap from anyone. But Price had a job to do and he knew it. There was no way he could let insubordination of that magnitude go without putting a stop to it.

"I'm demoting you to an E1, docking your pay, and you have latrine duty for 30 days."

"Yes, sir. Thank you, sir. I don't know what got into me. It musta been the sun."

"It was the sun alright, soldier. I'd better not ever see you in the med tent with a sunburn. Inside the wire, strip down as much as you want. Outside, full cover."

"Yes, sir. Thank you, sir."

The Colonel had the Company Commander in next. "I'm removing you from command. You seem incapable of maintaining discipline. In a war zone, that can cost lives. I need a prick running that company."

"Like Dobbs, sir?"

"Yeah, like Dobbs."

As the former company commander left, Price wondered if maybe it wouldn't behoove him to spend more time in the field with the soldiers. See what was going on. There needed to be two of him. One to go to meetings and do desk work, the other to carry a weapon. One to be a nice guy, the other a prick.

Starbuster

Bravo Company was doing route clearance in a little town called Al-Karmah. The route clearance was for the Marines who were going to put a command center right in the middle of Al-Karmah, in an abandoned house. The townspeople weren't too happy about the Marines being there in the first place, let alone building a command center right in the middle of their town. Colonel Price just shook his head. All of the work the Guard put into public relations and the Marines had to pull a power play. The Iraqis didn't know the difference between Active Duty Marines and the National Guard. It was like, "Up yours, American Yankee Fucks."

Bravo Company was supposed to clear a route into the city to ensure there were no IED's. It was a routine mission, if there was such a thing as "routine." Colonel Price was having his doubts.

All of a sudden, on Blue Force Tracker, there was a text message that a woman civilian had been wounded. "Uh, oh." Price was dumbstruck. "How-in-the-fuck does that happen?" He was about to find out.

Jeremy Atkins was in the lead Humvee of the route clearance team and had been trying to stop traffic because they'd found an IED that they wanted to remove. The traffic wouldn't stop and people were getting closer and closer, so he shot off a starbuster. Starbusters make a lot of noise and are used to scare people. Only the starbuster misfired and hit a pregnant lady right in the gut and it detonated. After it detonated it made a lot of noise and shot off flares. The woman was curled up on the ground, holding her stomach, writhing and coughing up blood.

The lieutenant from Bravo Company came running, picked the woman woman up, and headed off down the street, the woman's arms and legs flailing. He'd seen a Red Cross sign on the door of a building. The husband and father of the woman were running after him. The lieutenant burst through the door with the woman in his arms. There was an Iraqi doctor there, with a tongue depressor and flash light, looking in a child's throat. The doctor looked at the lieutenant and then at the woman. She was bleeding profusely and holding her stomach. The doctor said with disgust, "Well, what did you American dogs do now?"

The lieutenant realized the little clinic was not prepared to handle trauma. He turned around with the woman and ran back to the humvee where he could call in a Medevac. The husband and father ran after him, shouting in Arabic.

The lieutenant laid her on the seat of the Humvee. There was quite a crowd of angry Iraqis gathered around. The father of the woman climbed up on the hood of the Humvee, screaming in Arabic at the lieutenant. He tore off his shirt and threw it at the lieutenant. The lieutenant, from Sunday school lessons as a boy, knew this was a bad sign, a very bad sign. He had his .50 caliber in his hand. He looked at the gun and then at the father. The father had his chin stuck out as if daring/wanting the lieutenant to shoot.

Instead, the lieutenant threw the .50 caliber down on the ground and started crying. "I'm sorry. I'm sorry." The father started crying, also. Then the whole crowd began wailing and moaning. The look on their faces spoke, "This is what these dumb-ass Americans do to us."

The woman was air lifted out, but died in route, from blood loss and shock. There was an investigation that didn't amount to much. It was ruled an accident. The division civilian officer asked Price what he knew of the situation. Colonel Price said,

"Well, whatever they say, it's probably true. We were 100% at fault."

"The Imam head of the Muslim Community wants us to come over and talk. You can translate that into they want money."

The civilian officer and Colonel Price went over with $10,000 cash and met with the husband, father, grandfather and Imam. They sat cross-legged on a camel hair rug, talked and drank strong tea. Muslims have a belief that everything that happens is the Will of God, of Allah. If it wasn't the Will of God, it wouldn't have happened. But they still wanted money and settled for $2,500 for the death of the mother. Women are not worth as much as men. The husband said, "But my wife was pregnant."

The Imam didn't miss a beat. "Was it a boy or girl?"

"Uh, boy," the grandfather said, before the father could speak. "Allah told us it was a boy."

The U.S. Government paid out the $10,000. Everyone was happy.

After the starbuster incident, Bravo Company started calling Al-Karmah, Bad Karma.

BMW

Colonel Price was in his office. It was about 8:30 at night. A convoy escort was getting ready to leave Camp Ramadi for a long mission all the way to the Jordanian border, which was something they did often. Price was looking out the window. It was dark, very dark. Soldiers were pissing on the tires of Humvees before they left, which they did for good luck, even the female medics — they had PUD's (Personal Urinary Devices), which enabled them to stand-up and urinate like a man. He could see one female medic he recognized, Chris Mitchel, demonstrating how she could write her name, "Chris," in the sand. Price shook his head, but decided he would say nothing about the peeing episode, although it was certainly a violation of Military Code of Conduct. The soldiers had to have their fun. He could hear exchanging gunfire outside the main gate, which was all very normal.

All of a sudden there was automatic weapon fire coming from the head of the convoy. It was 451 fire, Price recognized the sound. "What the hell?" he said out loud. They had hardly gotten out of the gate. Radios fired up. Command wanted to know what was going on. Price climbed in his non-tactical Gator and told the driver to take him to the front of the convoy. Just then over the radio came, "It's a BMW. Uh, we have some civilians hit."

"Oh, shit!"

He told the driver to punch it.

When he arrived at the head of the convoy, there was a scene he would see in his dreams over and over again in the years to come. A black and yellow BMW was smoking at the side of the road, with bullet holes all through it. There was a fat man, outside of the car, the car door was open, one tire was flat, and the fat man had a bullet hole in his gut. He had his finger in the bullet hole to stop the bleeding. He was looking with a blank look at the soldiers, first at his gut, and then at them, and asking "Why?"

Medics were rushing to the car. There was a woman in the front seat. She was hit also. And there were kids in the back seat. At least one of them was hit.

The Lieutenant ran up to Price. "Uh, this car was coming up on us fast from the rear, like 80-miles an hour. The gunner thought it was a VBIED (Vehicle Born IED) and fired into the pavement to make it stop. It didn't. It started to pass. The gunner drilled it, which he's supposed to do. These people are crazy around here! It was a car full of civilians. We aborted mission."

Translators were talking to the man. He was a German. He looked just like an Iraqi. They were on vacation in Iraq, the bloodiest war zone in the world, to see his parents.

Price felt a sick feeling swoop through him. "You gotta be shitting me," was all he said to the Lieutenant, but knew there was going to be hell to pay.

There was hell to pay. To the tune of two-million U.S. dollars. The fat man died, but the wife survived to collect. One of her children was maimed for life. The German Consulate raised hell with the U.S. Embassy in Baghdad. They wanted money. The division civilian officer wanted Price to sign off on it.

"Time out here," Price told him. "What about personal responsibility? Everyone knows you don't pass a convoy, in a war zone, when shots are fired in front of you. Are they stupid or what?"

The civilian officer smacked himself in the forehead with his fist, and sighed. "Dude, just sign the fucking papers. The problem will go away."

The problem went away.

School Supplies

Different elements of the 451, like convoys and supply trucks, passed through the little village of Zamora, west of Baghdad, on a regular basis. It was a safe place to stop and rest, refuel, and just hang out. For some reason the insurgency left Zamora alone. It was either because the village leaders of Zamora were strong and resisted the insurgency, or because the insurgency just plain didn't give a rip about Zamora. There was no tactical or logistical advantage to be had in Zamora by the insurgency or, for that matter, the United States Military. It was just sort of a stopping over place, like an Interstate Rest Area. The only thing lacking, Colonel Price noted, were hand dryers at the piss holes. This was a joke, of course. Since the insertion of women into combat zones, the men could no longer use piss tubes — a plain, two inch pipe stuck in the sand that the men openly pissed into. Porta potties had to be installed. This created a whole new nightmare of distribution, handling and maintenance.

The U.S. Military would have liked to employ Iraqis for the unpleasant job of maintaining the porta potties, but it was feared the porta potties would also be an ideal place to plant a bomb. Put a bomb down the hole, wait until someone is using the porta pottie, then push a button on a cordless phone, and kablooey, another dead U.S. soldier, or two, depending on what the porta pottie was being used for. Porta potties were also a somewhat risky, but private, place to meet and do whatever. Hastily.

The people of Zamora were dirt (or sand) poor. They had very little of what might be considered modern conveniences. Televisions were rare, maybe one out of ten families had one.

And the ones that were present had to use rabbit-ear antennas, often draped with tinfoil or odds-and-ends of wire. An antenna on a roof would be sure to draw the eyes of insurgents who hated the spread of Western technology.

Colonel Price, on a tour of Zamora, noted that classrooms were segregated—the girls attended in the morning and the boys in the afternoon. He also noted the deplorable conditions of the classrooms. The children had very few school supplies. A stub of pencil was often shared by three-or-four students, and paper was so scarce that not an inch was left to waste. He wondered if the 451 could help with school supplies.

He hesitated. The school supplies could be used as a reward for the village's resistance to the insurgency, or it could be seen by the insurgency as a reason to attack the schools: the insurgency didn't want children educated (knowledge is power), especially the girls. Price was caught between a rock and a hard place.

However, the military had trained him that inaction is worse than wrong action. He decided to see what he could do, and let the bocce ball bounce wherever it may. If the insurgency used school supplies as a reason to punish the villagers, he would provide protection, and hope he wasn't too late.

He contacted some of his influential friends back in the states—school superintendents, pastors and business CEO's—explained the situation, asked for help—and then stood back and watched the magic happen. He involved as many of the 451's soldiers as he could so that they could see the rewards of supplying the needy with tools of education.

He was specific in what he wanted: backpacks, pencils, sharpeners, crayolas, chalk, finger paint, ink pens, tablets, notebooks, etc. He knew backpacks were a tricky item in Iraq—they could be used to carry explosives and ammunition. But he also knew he had to take a risk. The higher the risk, the greater the reward.

A whole cargo plane full of school supplies landed at the airport in Baghdad. It then had to be transported overland to Zamora by truck. Once again, it was tricky business. The convoy trucks were prime targets for insurgents placing IED's. Miraculously, the trucks made it through. Price wondered if it was the hand of God clearing the way, or Dingman and Jones and their computers. Price was a church-going man, yes, but not necessarily a great believer. He saw religion as a moral compass, teaching right and wrong, and providing a guide for living. The spiritual aspect he had never seen direct evidence of. He might have to revise his thinking.

On the day supplies were delivered to the school, he had as many soldiers helping out as he could muster. They were getting in each others' way, but the looks on the Iraqi children's faces, when they saw the school supplies, were priceless. They had never seen such a bounty of anything, let alone school supplies. They began immediately to write and draw on the tablets and notebooks and to fill their backpacks with supplies.

Price heard the teacher say in English, "Americans are very wealthy. They give this to you so that you can learn and be like them."

Price didn't know if this was a warning or a compliment.

"Gee, Colonel," one of the soldiers said to him. "I hated school when I was their age. Shows-to-go-you. Deny someone something and they want it all the more."

Colonel Price spit on the sand, although he didn't chew tobacco. He found chewing tobacco a nasty habit. "We're not going to win the war with guns and fighting," he told the soldier, "but education and voting will move mountains."

"Can I quote you on that, Colonel?"

Price turned around. It was a reporter from Reuters.

Colonel Price almost said, "You fuck'n-A," but caught himself. Instead he said, "You Goddamned right."

Cameras were rolling. Where they came from, or how they knew what was happening, he had no idea.

The next day he was talking to his wife on one of their rare telephone link-ups. She said, "I saw the 451 distributing school supplies to Iraqi children on CBS last night. I think I saw you in the background. I'm so proud of you, Bert. I wish you were here. I'd screw the socks off you."

Colonel Price was so horny he couldn't see straight. Even the Iraqi women, fully covered, were becoming attractive. He considered phone sex with his wife, but overcame the urge. The phone enclosures they had weren't all that private. So, instead he said, "You know? Seeing the school supplies distributed to those poor kids was one of the rare moments I was actually happy right where I was at, and wasn't thinking about home and you and the kids. Those Iraqi children deserve an education, every bit as much as ours do. Here's the good part: not a dollar of those school supplies was paid for by the U.S. tax payer. It was all donations. I'm proud of my America."

Of course, there were far too many school supplies to be distributed all at once. The majority of the supplies had to be warehoused and saved for a latter date. When the warehouse was broken into and the contents stolen, Price, as well as the U.S. Military were baffled. The insurgency would normally have burned the contents in a public display of power and hate.

An investigation of the incident revealed that it was indeed the insurgency who broke into the warehouse. But apparently they were stealing the supplies for themselves and their children.

"Well, I'll be go-to-hell," Colonel Price said, taking off his camo hat and wiping his forehead with a hankie. "Maybe those supplies are answering a higher calling. There may be a God after all."

Newsletters

Colonel Price, with his BA and MA degrees in English, was quite a prolific newsletter writer. He sent these newsletters — about what the 451 Engineering Battalion was doing — back to the families of soldiers and other interested entities, such as newspapers and radio stations. Colonel Price was a beautiful writer and obviously enjoyed the art of writing and, for the most part, the newsletters were well received and looked forward to by the people back home.

His newsletters were not without controversy, however, and it's a little curious as to why military command let him get away with such free-wheeling, over exposing, possibly dangerous writing. Loose lips sink ships.

The soldiers were drilled and drilled as to what they could and could not say in their phone calls, emails and letters back home. "Sorry, Hon. I can't tell you where we're going or what we will be doing because it's classified. If the enemy gets wind of it, it could cost lives."

However, Price just laid it right out there: what their mission was, where they were going and what was expected of them. Some spouses refused to read the newsletters because they were revealing more information than their own spouse was allowed to share, while other spouses welcomed the communiques as being informational and well written. Price did have a gift for writing, that varied from overly stiff, to poetic, to clownish.

Writing newsletters was also a relief valve for Colonel Price. He was plagued with insomnia and would spend many a night writing newsletters. It helped him relax. Like many writers, putting his thoughts down on paper was a form of organization. By writing it out, he could often make sense out of what was otherwise, chaos. And he enjoyed and thought it creative to be able to put a positive spin on what was really, sometimes, tragic bloodshed. He was the 451's biggest cheerleader. He was the National Guard's great communicator.

6-1-07

Dear wives, husbands, friends, families and followers of our soldiers. I am pleased to announce that one of our missions of escorting/transporting the giant MOAG, (Mother of All Generators) cross country is moving along, slow, but steady. It's top speed is a mind-boggling 5 mph, and is typically 2-3 mph. Boredom is more challenging than clearing IED's in front of the MOAG.

The behemoth generator — Mother of All Generators — when up and running will supply Iraq with 6% of its electrical needs — a big boon to Iraqis and a tremendous PR boost for the U.S. However, because of its size and importance, MOAG is also a prime target for insurgents (Mother of All Targets) who do not want to see it delivered, let alone operating — if they understand what it's for. We are constantly sniped at, have rockets shot at us and countless IED's placed in our path. Thank God for the Buffalo, a giant mine sweeping vehicle with an arm that reaches out, picks up the IED and detonates it, sometimes with harmful effects to the operators of the Buffalo, such as concussions and hearing loss, even with ear protection. We actually have a picture of an IED detonating. It is an awesome sight — purple, red, green. The soldier who snapped the shot (I do not have his name) was Johnny on the spot (also lucky)!

I wish to remind everyone of the radio broadcasts every Saturday morning at 0900 on Grover FM station 98.3. During these broadcasts, the commentator, Delwin McMulin, will be interviewing someone from the 451. This coming Saturday it will be yours truly talking about our mission, the morale of the troops, and any possible causalities.

I regret to say that we have had casualties, but this is war, and soldiers as well as civilians will be injured and even killed. Be assured to know that every possible measure, procedure and precaution is being taken to keep your loved one safe and secure.

May God bless you all for your effort at home. We realize this deployment is as hard, maybe harder, on you at home as it is on us in Iraq. With God's guidance and mercy, we will prevail, be home in the future, with mission accomplished.

{{{{{{{{{{{{{{{{************}}}}}}}}}}}}}
{{{{{{{{{{*****Signed*****}}}}}}}}}}}
{{{{{{{{{{{{{{{************}}}}}}}}}}}}}}}}

Bert M. Price
Colonel, Engineer
Commanding

1

---

1   It's an interesting affectation or quirk or even a fetish of Colonel Price that he spent the time to decorate his valediction with brackets and asterisks. It may be a form of doodling, using a keyboard rather than paper and pencil. It is very character revealing. Colonel Price is a detail person to the point of being anal-retentive. For a Colonel in charge of 500 soldiers to spend the time doodling his name in this manner, something I the author have never ever seen before, speaks volumes. Of course, he no doubt had the "artwork" saved, so that all he had to do was paste it. But still, what is the significance, or what does it say about the Colonel when he signs his name in this manner? Is it self-aggrandizement or narcissism or a coping mechanism? You be the judge.

7-28-07

Dear wives, husbands, friends, families and followers of our soldiers. I want to send a shout-out to the county Cattlemen Associations of NE Iowa. They pooled their money and beef processing resources to send the 451 in Iraq over 300 lbs of tasty beef sticks. Yummy. We do appreciate the protein, and the beef sticks compliment our MRE's (Meals Ready to Eat) which can become tasteless and boring. However, we do use the plastic bags the MRE's come in for other purposes, like defecation containers while in the field.

We also use the beef sticks for other purposes besides our personal consumption. They make excellent give aways to the Iraqi people, especially the children, who are often protein challenged. Chocolate is great, but in this 110 – 130 degree heat, chocolate isn't practical because it melts. Beef sticks, on the other hand, in their plastic wrap and natural preservatives, like salt and spices, in this dry heat, hold up well, and are easy to hand out. They're like waving little magic wands. And it is a type of magic to see the good they do.

We have to be careful, however. It was noted that one little Iraqi boy, who was quite sneaky in collecting a number of these beef sticks, became sick, and was vomiting after consuming maybe as many as a dozen beef sticks at one time. Becoming sick, even though he gorged himself on too many, makes the Iraqi children, and general population, suspicious that the beef sticks are bad and that the U.S. troops are trying to poison them. I have instructed our soldiers to try their best to not give out more than one or two beef sticks per child or adult. It is difficult however, because of the confusion of handing out food to malnourished people, and the conundrum that they all look alike.

The problem seems to be taking care of itself. 300 lbs of beef sticks distributed to over 500 troops didn't really last all that long — less than a week, actually. We do appreciate the efforts of the county Cattlemen's Associations, and the beef sticks were a nice treat for the troops and the people of Iraq. Myself personally, I found the beef sticks to remind me a lot of Iowa and home. Beef sticks were always easy to pick up at convenience stores when traveling and as an add-on for lunches. My mother always put a beef stick in my lunch when I was detasseling for Pioneer Seed Corn as a teenager. Sandwiches might become soggy, but not beef sticks!

We in the 451 hope all is well on the home front. We know that it is a burden on the family for us to not be there. There are all kinds of tasks that we performed that now must be accomplished by the folks at home, like mowing, cleaning the gutter and servicing vehicles. Be sure to utilize the 451's home services, and the family organizations that are in place to assist you. They are a Godsend.

Keep us in your prayers, and we will also pray for you. May God bring us home safely, and may you be patient in awaiting the arrival of your beloved soldier.

{{{{{{{{{{{{{{{{{************}}}}}}}}}}}}}}}
{{{{{{{{{{*****Signed*****}}}}}}}}}
{{{{{{{{{{{{{{{{************}}}}}}}}}}}}}}}}

Bert M. Price
Colonel, Engineer
Commanding

9-5-07

Dear wives, husbands, friends, families and followers of our soldiers. 9/11 is approaching fast, and we with the 451 are on high alert, as the insurgents may use this anniversary to launch a major attack. All furloughs have been canceled and *extra guards have been placed at check points and on perimeter towers around the base, if you can call this a base. It's more of a staging area or dumping ground for our operations.*

We will also honor 9/11 with a broadcast from our great Commander-in-Chief, President George W. Bush, to the troops. All available soldiers will muster in the parade field (If you can call it that) for the broadcast. We never want to forget why we are here. On September 11, 2001, the evil forces of Osama bin Laden viciously attacked the United States and destroyed the Twin Towers, and attempted to destroy the Pentagon and our U.S. Capital. The heroic efforts of a few brave people on an ill-fated flight, fighting bare handed, probably saved our capital. We honor those brave men and women by performing our duty in this Godforsaken Hell Hole to the utmost of our ability. Freedom is not free. It takes sacrifices from soldiers and civilians alike to eradicate the vermin that is trying to take down our capitalist democracy.

An "atta boy" or Impact Award goes out to Spec Scot Victor, from Grover, Iowa for his herculean and gymnastic endeavors in stringing communication lines between palm trees and our command structures. Untrained in electrical wiring, he took on the task without question or complaint. In the absence of a bucket truck, Spec Victor was lifted to necessary heights by a cherry picker attached to his belt, exposing himself to sniper attack. The belt broke and Spec Victor fell to the ground, on his back, knocking the wind out of him. Once he regained his breath, he reattached the cherry picker to his belt and back up he went. (Of course he did some cussing.) This is the type of effort and can-do attitude that will win this war, and for which Spec Victor received a Challenge Coin. Good job, Specialist Victor.

The best news I saved for last. As you know, the 451 Engineering Battalion is attached to a Marine Infantry Division.

It is the 451's responsibility to provide engineering support for the Marines: i.e.: build bridges and roads, clear IED's and build necessary structures as needed. In short, because the 451 enters the war zone or battlefield in advance of the infantry soldiers, we actually do the bulk of the fighting. The Marines won't admit this, but it's true. It has just been announced that the 451 will be able to attach the Marine's shoulder patch to our uniforms. This has only been allowed very rarely in military history. For a National Guard Unit to wear the insignia of an Active Duty Marine Infantry battalion, shows their utmost respect for us. We consider it to be the highest honor that the Marines could pay to the 451, and we will wear the Marine shoulder patch with pride.

Our thoughts and prayers go out to our families and loved ones back home. We know that our service is also your service, only we get recognition for it. Maintain the highest level of confidentiality as to what the 451's mission is, and we will return, hopefully by the end of the year, in time for Christmas. May God be with you all.

{{{{{{{{{{{{{{{{*************}}}}}}}}}}}}}}}}
{{{{{{{{{{{*****Signed*****}}}}}}}}}}}
{{{{{{{{{{{{{{{{*************}}}}}}}}}}}}}}}}

Bert M. Price
Colonel, Engineer
Commanding

Colonel Price would receive recognition and an award for his communication skills, most notably the newsletters. He was never reprimanded for divulging sensitive information, and no known casualties or injuries were tied directly to his communiques.

He keeps the bundle of newsletters in his file and every once-in-a-while, he gets them out and looks through them. And remembers.

He was asked by several of his soldiers, since he was such a good writer, if he would write a book about the 451's deployment in Iraq. He declined, saying he didn't want to relive all that they had gone through. Some of the soldiers spit on words such as that, saying, "What did he go through? He did paperwork while we got our ass blown off!"

On the ten-year anniversary of the 451's deployment, he re-sent out the stack of newsletters to everyone who had been on the original distribution—the ones who were still alive. Some people enjoyed them, some ignored them, and some threw them in the trash.

The 451 would go on to earn Top Battalion Award in 2011 with Colonel Bert Price listed as the Commanding Officer.

Going Home

The National Guard battalion that replaced the 451 in 2008 was from Georgia, an infantry battalion. They were about the same size, but being infantry, as opposed to combat engineers, there was constant friction and rivalry between the two that could escalate to counter productive measures: not good for the overall mission of fighting terrorism. Combat engineers thought they did all the work but got little credit, where infantry thought they were the real fighting force.

The 451 was to leave all of their equipment and supplies behind and take literally nothing with them except what they were wearing. The Georgia Brigade came in with a full supply of everything: vehicles (fully armored Dwight noticed), weapons, munitions, supplies, new computers, the works. What this did was create a glut of military equipment that would not be used. "There's something wrong with this picture," Dwight thought. "What a waste." It was then he began thinking that Powell's All-Volunteer-Army, and rotating National Guard units in and out, might not be the best way to fight a war. "When this was over, and it will be over some day," Dwight was thinking, "where will all this equipment go?" Into the hands of the enemy, was the logical answer, just like Vietnam.

Each soldier in the Iowa unit was assigned his or her replacement from the Georgia unit. The Iowa soldier would train the Georgia soldier in his or her job for one week, then the Georgia soldier would take over for the second week, while the Iowa soldier observed. Two weeks to transfer knowledge, power and pride. Theoretically it should work. In reality, there were problems, hurdles too high to jump, or to pole vault over. Dwight called it, "Pole vaulting over mouse turds."

Dwight's replacement was a young, brash college graduate (computer science) who thought the algorithms Dwight was writing to predict the placement of IED's was rudimentary and non-functional. He didn't express it in so many words, but Dwight could tell from his body language that he just wanted Dwight out of there, and that he was going to do it his way. Dwight wanted to tell him that miscalculation and over confidence could get people killed, but knew the Georgia soldier was going to have to learn it the hard way, as Dwight had. Which was a shame. There was a learning curve that equated to soldiers lives.

Jeremiah was his name—Jeremy for short. Jeremy asked, "Where did you go to college?"

"I didn't," Dwight said. "OJT."

"Oh."

Dwight could have strangled the young punk. He was going to get people killed, Dwight knew it. But what could he do?

"You and Captain Dingman developed this program of predicting IED placement based on what?" Georgia wanted to know. (Dwight just called him Georgia.)

"Repetition. The terrorists follow the same pattern day-in, day-out, for the most part, or 80% of the time. They'll return to the same spot to place their IED whether it was successful the day before or not. It's part of their culture. Allah told me to put it here."

"And you learned this where?"

"From observation and our translators schooled us on how Muslims think."

"And you trust them?" Georgia was incredulous.

Georgia had a point. Dwight didn't completely trust the

translators. They could be working for both the Americans and the terrorists. But Dwight didn't particularly like being told something he already suspected, especially from Georgia.

"Look, fucker," Dwight was losing his patience. "Two of our translators were beheaded, and left for us to see. What does that tell you?"

Georgia's mouth dropped open. He was speechless. The war had just gotten real for him, too. Which was a good thing.

It took three days (nights) to chopper the 451 out of Ramadi to Baghdad. For some reason, Dwight never did know why, he was on the last chopper out on the last night. "Story of my life," he told Hunziker, the soldier next to him. "Hurry up and wait."

Even though he was on the last bird out, they all had to be on the landing pad at all times. That was in case something happened, and in Ramadi, something always happened.

Waiting was hard on everybody. Fights broke out, over the most trivial things, like, "Hey, motherfucker. That's my Playboy. I was taking it home to show my wife what I want her to do when I get there."

"Naw, that ain't your Playboy. You had that scratch-and-sniff Penthouse. If you want your wife to smell like that, why don't you scratch between your asshole and dick. That's what your wife's cunt smells like."

The fight that ensued over that conversation involved about a dozen soldiers, and it took Dwight, two other non-coms, an officer and the Colonel to break it up. One soldier looked like he had a broken nose, another had a couple of teeth knocked out. One of the 451's medics, Chris Mitchel, attended to them. Either one of them could have had a concussion, but there weren't any x-ray machines on the tarmac. They would have to tough it out.

Colonel Price was PO'd. "Jesus Christ you guys. We're on

our way home and now I'm gonna have to reprimand you and deal with you when we get to Ft. Sill. You're gonna look real awkward at that 'welcome home' in Erkson, busted down to a private. Can't you be civilized for once?"

"Sorry, Colonel, but Sloan disrespected my wife."

"Shi,"chided Sloan. "Your wife Johned you six months ago. She's fuck'n your best friend. Remember?"

The fight just about reignited. It would have if a chopper hadn't landed, taking everybody's attention off what was happening on the ground. They all wanted on that bird.

Dwight was nervous. It was 0430, just starting to get light. It was called BNT—Before Nautical Twilight. Dwight knew damned well what happened when it was light. They would be shot at. If you fly during the daylight, you're going to get shot at—period, end of story.

The Blackhawk held 14 soldiers. The last 14. Dwight was strapped in, just wanting to get the hell out of there, fast. The pilot took the bird to full military power. It shuddered like it was going to rattle apart, and then they shot into the air.

Dwight could see out of one side portal. The sun was just beginning to poke its head up in the east, like the rim of a golden crescent. There was irony in that for Dwight—a golden, sunlight on such a shitty, dangerous city — the most dangerous city in the world, actually.

There was a flash on the ground. It was a tracer. They were being shot at! Dwight thought, "This is it. We ain't even going to make it out of Ramadi." The soldier beside him had his hands clasped together, praying. Dwight could hear his words, "The Lord is my Shepherd, I shall not want." The pilot knew what he was doing and banked hard to the left in an evasive maneuver, almost putting the chopper into a roll, which would have been the end for them all. But the ground to air rocket, probably Russian, went over the top.

The soldiers broke out in cheers. The pilot spoke into their headsets, "Courtesy of Air Ramadi. You can leave my tip with the flight attendant."

The soldiers all laughed.

Dwight knew they had escaped a close one. If there was another, they might not be so lucky.

At Baghdad, there were two Australian Jumbo Jets waiting. The military always contracted with the lowest bidder. It took another two days of waiting on a hot tarmac before they were all loaded and ready to fly. At night again. Dwight never knew he could be so tired, stinky, and sweaty.

But they got loaded and the Aussie pilot backed the Jumbo Airplane down the runway until the back wheels dropped off the tarmac. He then inched back on to the hard surface, held the brakes, revved the engines to full power, and they went flying down the runway. Dwight could see the lights at the end of the runway approaching fast. He didn't think they were going to make it. At the last second, the pilot pulled the stick back, and they shot almost straight up into the air. Dwight was pinned to the back of his seat and couldn't even turn his head to look out the window. If they were a target, he didn't want to know.

But they leveled off and the lights of Baghdad disappeared. Many of the soldiers held their middle finger to the window.

It was a 12-hour flight across the ocean. Most of the soldiers, including Dwight, were asleep, or what passed for sleep. It was just a dark numbing sensation, full of bad dreams of what they had been through in the last year, and hopes for a better life ahead. It helped pass the time. Little did they know that the life they were flying into might not be as easy as the one they left behind. Struggles at home could be harder to deal with than IED's, rockets and insurgents.

Dwight, with his eyes closed, thought he smelled something hot, like electrical-fire fumes. He kept his eyes closed and rubbed his finger across his nose. He thought it might be part of the dream he was having. He drifted back into the dark hole. He could see the three marines on fire, that's what he smelled—burning bodies—and Eddie Beams with the top of his head sheared off.

He smelled it again—some kind of hot electrical insulation burning somewhere. His eyes popped open. Other soldiers were coming out of their delirium and smelling it too. "What the fuck?" they were saying. Dwight's mind shot back to his training as a Nuclear Biological Chemical Specialist. Bleach! Panic gripped him. He had to act fast or they would all be dead! Where was his chemical suit? Oh, he was on an airplane. Smoke was coming out of a vent. The plane was on fire! They were all going to be killed! They were going to crash into the ocean never to be found! He couldn't believe he had just gone through a hell-war, only to be killed on his way home. He was not going to let that happen! But what could he do?

The copilot and a flight attendant were running out of the cockpit—one down each aisle. They were headed for the back bathroom. "Make a hole!" they were hollering in their Aussie accent. "We gotta fire in the back water closet."

They got to the back and pulled the door open. The bathroom was full of smoke. They were coughing and didn't seem to know what to do. Dwight headed back like a charging bull. He pushed the two out of the way, ripped the false ceiling apart, and tore the fan out with his bare hands. He then threw it in the chemical toilet. There was a little fire extinguisher hanging beside the towel dispenser, he grabbed it, and doused the fan motor with foam.

He looked at his hands. There were some nasty burns and blisters forming.

"Looks like you burned your 'ands, Mate," one Aussie said. "Ere, we got a first aid kit."

The soldiers cheered Dwight. Medic Chris Mitchel pushed the Aussies out of the way, slathered Neosporin on Dwight's hands, and bandaged him. "You saved us, Dwight," she said. "This could've been really bad if that fire had gotten out of control."

At Ft. Sill, nine out-of-ten 451 soldiers departing the airplane, including Dwight, kissed the ground. They weren't home. But they were in the U.S. of A!

Ft. Sill couldn't have been a worse place. It was an artillery training ground, and there were pops, bangs and explosions going off night and day. The 451 soldiers spent as much time hitting the ground as they did standing in line for discharge physicals and mental evaluations. Their nerves were shot. Going home was supposed to be a peaceful, happy occasion. Instead it was a nightmare of flashbacks, bad dreams and mundane paperwork.

Colonel Price held his hearing for the soldiers involved in the fight in Ramadi. He hated to do it, but discipline had to be maintained, even going home. He busted two soldiers down to E1's and docked the pay of a couple others.

"Prick to the end," he heard one of them say on the way out.

"Yeah," he said to himself. "Price the prick."

Welcome Home!

Erkson Police Officer, Jocko Mitchel, sat in his squad car at a pull-over on Highway 16 outside of Grover, waiting for 451's buses to appear. Also at the pullover was a deputy sheriff. They were waiting to escort the returning 451 Combat Engineers to Erkson where a welcome home ceremony would take place at the high school gymnasium. Jocko and the deputy played rock-paper-scissors to determine who would lead the procession. Jocko won. Rock breaks scissors.

Jocko's nuts hurt. His wife, Chris, was on one of those buses, he didn't know which one. She had been gone 13 months.

Another Erkson police officer had bid on the escort job, and because of seniority, he should have been awarded the privilege. But the Police Chief said, "Naw. Jocko's wife is on one of those buses. By God Jocko gets the job."

Jocko chewed on his fist. Tears formed. Chris was coming home.

He saw the buses coming over the hill. He turned on his red lights and got in front of the lead bus. Everybody better clear a path, his wife was on one of those buses! There were cars pulled over to the side of the road and people waving. On the outskirts of town, the Erkson Fire Department had stationed their ladder truck. The ladder was fully extended with a huge American Flag hanging down over the street.

When the soldiers saw that, cheers erupted on the bus. All pain and suffering of the last 13 months were swept away in a wave of patriotism, pride and a vision of glory to come.

When Jocko saw Chris in her clean and pressed camo uniform, he couldn't believe his eyes. It wasn't that she looked older—she looked more mature. Maybe wiser? They hugged and kissed, and it was good to feel her melt into the soft spots of his body. "Never leave me again," he told her.

"No problem there," She said.

They commenced having children.

Dwight's wife, Virginia, who hadn't deployed with him and was now out of the Guard, was recording the whole event. She knew what was about to take place. Dwight didn't.

Of course, all the triumphs, tragedies and accolades of the 451's deployment were highlighted by Colonel Price: over 800 IED's removed or detonated, free democratic elections set up for the first time in Iraq (albeit shaky), children provided with school supplies, and of course, four soldiers dead. They were listed by name, which wasn't necessary because their names were on big banners hanging from the ceiling. The medals and decorations awarded during the deployment were also listed.

"There's one more award I want to hand out," Colonel Price announced. "Would Sergeant Dwight Jones please step forward."

Dwight looked around. He wasn't sure he heard correctly. The other soldiers pushed him forward. He stood at attention.

Colonel Price walked up to him. They saluted, Dwight with a bandaged hand. "Sergeant Jones," Colonel Price barked loud enough for the whole auditorium to hear. "For outstanding work above and beyond the call of duty, for helping develop software to assist in finding the location, removal and detonation of over 800 IED's, which saved countless lives, I now present you with the U.S. Army's Bronze Star."

Dwight nearly fainted. He had been so disappointed that he

hadn't received the Bronze Star while in Iraq. Captain Dingman had. Dwight was bitter that others had received recognition and medals, while he hadn't. He had worked just as hard as anyone, probably harder, and helped accomplish something the entire U.S. Army hadn't been able to do. To get the Bronze Star now, in front of all these people, many of whom knew him, well, he was totally unprepared. Dwight couldn't help it, but tears formed, and then he was bawling, rubbing his fists in his eyes, and wiping snot from his nose with the back of his hand.

"Get a grip, Dwight," Colonel Price whispered. "Show this auditorium some National Guard pride."

Virginia, Dwight's wife, had it all on film. She scowled a little. Dwight had gained weight while in Iraq.

Captain Dobbs, in the back of the formation, bit his lip. He said to himself, "Yeah, Herman Stein and John Washington thank you very much, you asshole."

There was something wrong. Virginia didn't seem to be as excited to see Dwight as Dwight was to see her. She seemed withdrawn, a little cold. Dwight was so horny he could have screwed a knothole, where Virginia seemed like she was performing a perfunctory duty. Going through the motions.

"What's wrong?" he asked her.

"Nothing, nothing. I'm just so proud of you. I don't know how to act."

Her words seemed hollow.

It was when he got the mail and there was a disconnect notice from the power company that his suspicions were heightened. Virginia, of course, took care of the bills while Dwight was gone, and he trusted her. He had always paid bills on time. A bill came, he paid it. End of story.

He asked her about the disconnect notice. "What's this?" he asked.

"Oh, give me that," she said. "I'll take care of it."

"Haven't you been paying the bills?" he asked.

"Of course, of course. It's got to be a mistake. Those people down at REA get things so screwed up. They have our bill mixed up with the neighbor's, that's all."

It was when he saw an outrageous credit card statement that he blew a gasket—he was having anger issues anyway (0-to-pissed off in three seconds). It was a joint credit card of Virginia's and his, and they owed over $30,000. The credit card company was turning it over to a collection company. Wage garnishments were forth coming.

"What the fuck is this?" Dwight asked.

Virginia's lower lip trembled. "Dwight, Dwight, I'm sorry. I'll make it up to you."

"Make what up to me?" He looked at the credit card statement. There were massive charges to something called Rocky Mountain Gemstone. "What's this gemstone bullshit?"

"They'll double in price in less than a year," she cried. "It's guaranteed,"

"Oh, Jesus Christ. Gemstones?"

Then the mortgage company called and said they were foreclosing on the house. Payments hadn't been made in over six months. Dwight went berserk. He grabbed Virginia by the arm. His face was so red that a vein in his forehead stood out like it would burst.

She clawed his face.

When he let go, she stomped out of the house, got in the car and left. She didn't return for three days. When he asked where she'd been, she just sort of snickered, gathered up her clothes and left again.

He found out later Virginia was living with a guy in another town. It was obvious that she had been seeing this person while Dwight was deployed. Dwight considered murder. He would grind up the bodies in his venison grinder and dispose of the contents in the Upper Iowa River. No one would know. He would then disinfect the grinder. He was a NBC expert and knew how to do these things.

He got drunk instead. For three days.

Dwight was forced to declare bankruptcy. They lost everything.

The divorce was even more bitter. He couldn't believe that part of his military pension was going to go to Virginia. Here he had been fighting a war to defend the country, while Virginia was fucking around, spending his money, and now he had to pay her! He was a war hero, by golly. His career in the military had been stellar. He was supposed to come home to a happy life of accolades, back slaps, and everything would be easy-peasy-lemon-squeezy compared to what he had been through. Instead it was worse than the hell in Iraq. At least in Iraq you knew who the enemy was. You didn't always see him, but you knew he was there.

A black cloud hung over everything, similar to when Herman Stein and John Washington had been killed. Alcohol, plus marijuana, plus speed, plus meth, plus Ecstasy, plus whatever-he-could-get-his-hands-on, helped blot out and deaden the pain, the nightmare. He kept getting nightmares mixed up—the one in Iraq, and the one at home.

He couldn't even remember picking the woman up at the

bar. But he woke up beside her in a sleazy motel. Her breath smelled like gasoline. He had to take her back to the bar where he picked her up the night before. She asked for money. He opened his wallet and it was empty. He showed it to her and she flipped him off. He decided as long as he was at the bar, he might as well have a drink. Or two. Or three. The bartender, who he knew from high school, let him run up a tab.

"Why don't you go easy there, Woodie," the bartender/friend said.

"Fuck you."

He came to on the grass in front of the house he was renting in the country. It was nearly noon. He had pissed his pants. He needed to have a bowel movement and considered doing it in his pants. He did.

Could anyone see him? His face was swollen from bug bites and his tongue felt like it was twice its size and made of cinder. He wanted to die. It would be easy, "Ha! Easy-peasy-lemon-squeezy again. A gun to his head, or mouth. Which one? Don't flinch, motherfucker! Carbon monoxide, downers? The choices were endless. Which one would be the less painful? Downers. Gobble'm down, go to sleep and never wake up. That was it. Where to get them? The bartender. That's right. His old high school buddy. Bartenders are always the biggest dealers, or know who is.

There was a little dog curled up beside him. Its name was Mitsy and was Virginia's dog, a dachshund. Mitsy was licking his face and whining.

Dwight rolled over and threw up. Mitsy sniffed and started to eat the vomit. Dwight grabbed her and held her to his chest. She continued to whine and nuzzle him in the neck with her nose.

"Okay, girl, okay" he said. "You're right. This is no way to act. I'm a Sergeant in the National Guard. You don't need to eat my vomit. I can eat it myself. I need help. I know I do."

He called the VA.

On the way to Rochester, Minnesota, to the VA, he considered driving his car head-on into an overpass. He was still intoxicated and so hungover he was seeing double. He closed one eye, aimed the car for the pillar and jammed the accelerator to the floor. The car stalled and died. He couldn't believe it. He couldn't even kill himself!

It took him an hour at the side of the road to drain the carburetor so the car would start. The engine had flooded when he jammed his foot to the floor. "Piece of shit!" he screamed at the vehicle, and kicked it. Some rusty metal fell off and busted on the ground.

He got behind the wheel and tried to start the car. It gasped, but gurgled to life. "Like me," Dwight said.

A Highway Patrolman stopped to see if help was needed. Smelling alcohol on Dwight's breath, and noticing his obvious disheveled appearance, he asked, "Have you been drinking, sir?"

"Who me?"

"Put your hands behind your back and turn around."

"Please, I'm a veteran. I'm a Sergeant in the National Guard. I just got back from Iraq. I'm headed for the VA. I need help."

"You need help alright. I'm in the Guard, too. You're a disgrace."

Dwight's one call from his jail cell was to the VA.
They sprung him.

The VA Counselor, a woman, asked. "Do you have dreams of what happened in Iraq?"

Dwight couldn't look at her. He held his head in his hands, and shook his head yes."

"Do you want to die?"

He wanted to deny it, but knew he had to stuff his pride and be honest. He shook his head yes again. For some reason, he didn't know why, he could express his feelings to a woman, where he couldn't a man.

"I think in-patient treatment is your best bet."

He spent 30 days. There were other veterans just like him, some of them from Vietnam and really old. They were all over weight and scruffy looking, with long, smelly beards that were stained yellow from nicotine—their fingers the same yellow, with long fingernails like a woman's.

Dwight was appalled, and wondered if that's what he was going to look like, or worse yet, if he looked like that now? He remembered from one of his earlier counseling sessions, the psychologist saying, "If you want to know who you are, look at who you run with."

In Group he told his story how he had gotten soldiers killed by giving them information that led them into a trap.

There was silence in the group; a couple of them, with their arms folded over their bellies, nodded their heads, in agreement.

One old vet, who had a pierced ear with a gold ring, and a face that looked like shoe leather, spat on the floor, although they were inside.

The counselor spoke up. "Fish Bait, that's enough. Let him talk."

"Fuck him," Fish Bait said, wiping his mouth with the back of his hand. "That ain't shit." He looked at Dwight. "Boy, you sandbox soldiers are pussies. We had foot rot from the jungle and maggots in our food. I saw Cong slitting pregnant Gooks' bellies open, ripping fetuses out, throwing them in the air and catching them on bayonets. I got three Cong before they got me. 18 months a POW. You think you had it rough?"

"It's all relevant, Fish Bait," the counselor said. "No cross talking."

Dwight was stunned.

In one-on-one with the counselor, she said, "Put those dead men in a boat, Dwight. They're floating down the river having a good time, drinking beer. It's a sunny day, and they're fishing. Wave at them, Dwight."

Dwight raised his right hand and waved.

"They're floating off into the sunset. Wave goodbye to them, Dwight."

Dwight waved good bye.

"Did they wave back, Dwight?"

Dwight nodded his head, yes. "They waved back."

OWI and Cancer

Now, on top of everything else—divorce, bankruptcy, wanting to die, and wondering what life is all about, and whether the U.S. involvement in the Middle East was worth it—Dwight had an OWI to deal with. His mind kept flashing back to the arrest and what the officer said, "You're a disgrace."

He was a disgrace. Dwight looked at himself in the mirror. He was overweight, his civilian clothes didn't fit him, his hair was long and greasy, his beard was growing out in tufts, and he had bags under his eyes. In short, he looked like one of those smelly, long-in-the-tooth veterans he didn't like the looks of. Was he going to get a nickname, like Fish Bait? (Whose real name was Fischbane.) Instead of Bright Dwight, would he be Blight Dwight or Fright Dwight? His troubled mind dug him deeper and deeper into a hole. His counselor had told him, "If you're in a hole, Dwight, stop digging." He couldn't stop digging.

The judge had little mercy, even though Dwight was a veteran. It was a routine $1,000 fine, three days in jail, loss of license, and high risk insurance for three years once he got his license back. His lawyer cost $5,000. What good she did, Dwight wasn't sure. However, the three days in jail gave him time to think. Sober.

When he checked into the county jail on a Friday night, there were a couple of other people checking in at the same time for the same offense. One of them was a woman. She had liquor on her breath and was obviously high and thought the whole ordeal was funny. The jailer didn't see the humor and promptly rearrested her for public intoxication. Her name was Brandy, which Dwight thought appropriate.

The county jail was also being used to handle overflow prisoners from Rochester who were waiting trial. One of them was a Devil Worshiper who had drawn evil, Satanic figures all over the jail-cell wall, and spent the daylight hours staring out of a tiny jail-cell window directly into the sun. He said he was getting messages from Satan. Dwight stayed away from him.

Another was a big, burly Afro American who claimed he had been drafted by the Green Bay Packers (Dwight believed him), and was in jail waiting a murder trial. He looked at Dwight like he wanted to chew Dwight up and spit him out. Dwight had been around a lot of tough people in the military, but he had to admit, this dude scared him. There was a scar across his forehead and cheek that was no-doubt caused from a knife slash. One ear lobe was missing. Dwight didn't even want to know how that happened. (Bit off?) His name was Rydel. He talked about himself in the second person, "Don't you boshit Rydel."

Rydel was the last person Dwight would have "boshitted."

A third person, a young white, effeminate male, was obviously gay or transgender, and made it clear to Dwight that he (or she) would accommodate Dwight in any manner he wanted. Dwight stayed clear of this person, also.

Dwight wanted nothing to do with these people. He wasn't one of them and didn't want them to think he was. He just wanted to serve his three days and get the hell out of that county jail. He spent his three days sitting on his bunk, trying not to draw the attention of these characters, and reviewed his life.

He remembered growing up on the river and learning the ways of the wild, which were the best life lessons he was ever taught, and applied directly to everyday living. He had read in Indian lore how wild game will actually give itself up to the starving hunter after a period of methodical stalking and praying. It had happened to Dwight several times, with various animals: deer, turkey, fox, even fish.

The first time it was a white tail buck Dwight had been tracking in the snow for three days. Dwight was dog tired, hungry (starving, actually) and at the point of giving up. He was following the buck's trail down to the river. He heard something, like breathing, and looked up. The buck was standing in front of him looking him right in the eye. It spoke to Dwight. "I give you my body for nourishment so you can become as me." The gun came to Dwight's shoulder and he dropped the buck. "Now eat my liver," it told him. Dwight cut open its belly and sliced out its liver. The wild taste in his mouth was of the forest and sky and river. Dwight was one with nature.

The same thing happened in everyday life. There were times when Dwight had searched and searched and prayed for something, then all of a sudden it was right in front of him, saying, "Take me." Algorithms spoke to him: "The IED is here."

He remembered studying the new machine called a personal computer in high school. It offered all the mystique and secrets and challenge of wild animals, and then some. "Give yourself up to me and we will become as one." He understood its language and spoke it, and they communicated.

He remembered his enlistment in the National Guard, three days after he had turned 17, with his parents permission. "Come and join us and we will take you around the world," it said to him. "We will show you the secrets of the Universe." Dwight wasn't sure he'd seen the Universe, but he knew he'd seen Hell. It wasn't pretty. He'd heard the, "Gnashing of teeth," like it talked about in the Bible.

He knew he had to get his life together, or end it. He had tried to end it, and it was like the hand of God preventing him. It was too uncanny how that car had stalled out when he aimed it at the overpass. He was alive for a reason.

"Wave goodbye to those men," the counselor told him.

Dwight raised his hand and waved. The effeminate person shot him a look. "Hey, Dude. Sup?"

"Fuck you," Dwight told him. "Don't even mess with me."

On Sunday morning, the "Three-day'rs" as they were called, those sentenced to three days in the slammer, were released early. It was Sunday morning and church bells were ringing. Dwight stood outside the county jail on the cement steps and looked at the pretty morning. He inhaled a deep breath of fresh air through his nostrils. He felt good, for a change. This was going to be a good day. He needed to take advantage of it. He was sober.

The girl, Brandy, was being let out at the same time. She stood on the jail steps also. Dwight looked at her. She didn't have that smirk on her face anymore. She looked like a limp noodle—a person who needed a hug.

"Wanna have breakfast?" he asked.

"Sure. Jail food fuck'n sucks, don't it?"

Over eggs, bacon, hashbrowns, orange juice and coffee, Dwight told her a little bit about himself. "Just got home from Iraq, found the wife shacking with another guy, divorce, bankruptcy. My life's a mess, don't know what I'm doing. I needed that OWI like I needed a hole in the head. But this is a pretty day. I'm taking it one day atta time."

Brandy looked at Dwight. She didn't know what to think. This guy was almost like a teddy bear, but smart, real smart. And the breakfast was good. What the hell? "I work for Case IH in Rochester," she said. "I gotta quit partying hearty. My bod won't take it anymore."

"I know what you mean."

Dwight took Brandy to his place. She liked his hairy chest. Dwight liked the thin blue veins he could see just beneath her milk white skin on her wrists. She was like a delicate butterfly.

"I got this idea for a business," he told her while lying in bed, staring up at the ceiling. "I'm pretty good with computers. Self taught, mostly. I'd like to work on people's computers, upgrade them, clean'm up, help people get set up with a home system. Maybe sell a few. Could call it Easy PC. What do you think?"

"Go for it."

"What's wrong?" Brandy asked Dwight. They had been living together for six months. Dwight's computer business was going gang busters, with people coming to him from all over with their computer problems, like they did in Iraq for safe, IED-free, routes. He went to clients' homes also, to install modems and Wifi's and alarm systems. He built computers per their specifications.

"I just feel so worn out lately, and my joints hurt—especially my knees and hips. And I dunno if you noticed, but my weight's get'n out-of-sight, no matter how little I eat."

"I noticed," she said, patting his belly. "Maybe you should see a doc. You go to the VA, don't cha?"

"Cancer of the thyroid," the VA doctor told him after running tests. "Were you exposed to anything while in the military?"

"You know? I was. There was an accident with Americium 241. It was in a canister in a detector unit run over by an Armored Personnel Carrier. Think big and heavy. It happened a couple of times. We were exposed to radiation. We knew it at the time but, hey, what do you do?"

"Well, I know what we're going to do," the doctor told him,

a pretty young woman. "That thyroid's going to come out and we're going to give you a couple of radiation treatments."

"You're going to treat a radiation-caused-cancer with radiation?" Dwight was a little aghast. It was sort of like the deer saying, "Eat my liver."

He checked with a couple of old Guard buddies who were present during that radiation exposure. Sure enough, one had a tumor on his pancreas, another, prostate cancer — both of which were much more serious than Dwight's. Dwight didn't know whether he should feel lucky or not. Cancer, yes. Treatable? Yes. Check, check. He supposed he could feel lucky.

Dwight noticed a peace-sign button on the doctor's lapel. "You a Peacenik?" Dwight asked, rather disgustedly.

Her blue eyes flashed, almost shooting sparks. "Damn straight. I had one brother, a fighter pilot, shot down over Nam, his body never recovered. Another brother with his legs blown off. All so our f'ing government can pull the hell out and leave those people dangling from helicopters, with not a damn thing accomplished. It's gonna be the same way in the Middle East. Mark my words."

"But they attacked the Trade Center. What the hell were we supposed to do, roll over?"

"You can't stop killing with killing."

"So, what's your solution?"

"Peace through education. Peace through food. Build them homes, give them fresh water. Peace through anything, but more killing."

"That's pretty pacifist talk, for a VA doc."

"That rhymes," she said, smiling. You a poet? Truth be known, most of the docs here are pacifists. They just keep a lid on it. I wear it on my sleeve, I mean my lapel. Ha! The higher the education, the less violence there is, sorta like the food chain."

Dwight was about to chide her but stopped. He knew well enough that what the 451 accomplished in Iraq, all those IED's found and disarmed, all those convoys gotten through safely, that the country of Iraq wasn't one iota better off than they were before the U.S. Military arrived. In fact, they might be worse. It was all such a waste of resources, time and effort, not to mention lives. You move the insurgents out of one country, they regroup in another, stronger than they were before. This wasn't like World War II or the Civil War where armies surrendered when defeated. The insurgents could fight a guerrilla war forever. Kill their leaders and next man up. This was like the Jews of old. Kill some of them off, it just spreads them further around the world. It was like pheasant hunting, which Dwight loved. The hunter is actually making the flock stronger by scaring them up and shooting at them, even killing a few. It spreads them out over a broader area for less inbreeding.

Dwight went home to Brandy. "I have some good news and I have some bad. What do you want first?"

Brandy held an index finger to her forehead. "Da, let's see, before I met you I was a bad news girl. I've changed. Gimmie me the good news first."

"Okay, well, what I have is 95% treatable."

"That's good. And the bad?"

"I do have cancer, of the thyroid. But with surgery, what they call a thyroidectomy, and a couple of radiation treatments, it's 95% treatable."

"That is good news, Dwight." She put her arms around him. "Oh, honey, I'm so happy since I met you. And to think, we met in jail!"

"On the steps leaving the jail. There's a difference. Nothing, absolutely nothing happens in God's world by accident." He had learned this from the little bit of AA he was exposed to in the VA.

"I have some news for you, too," Brandy tweeted, like a pretty little bird.

"Good or bad?"

"Good. Definitely good."

"Okay, let's have it." Dwight was looking at her (Brandy was much shorter than him) through the bottom lens of his trifocal glasses, making his eyes look super big, a look she adored because Dwight did have pretty brown eyes.

"I'm pregnant."

Dwight stepped back and held Brandy at arm's length. His vision of her moved to the center lens, where he studied her. "Wow. That is good news. I'll be a daddy?"

"Yup. And me a mama."

Dwight stammered, "Maybe we should tie the knot?"

"Ya think?"

Colonel Bert Price, Retired

E arlier, waiting on the tarmac to load up and go home, Colonel Price was picking his teeth. He had saved back a couple of beef sticks from the Cattleman's giveaway, and was eating them while waiting. Eating something helped kill time (something that would put excess weight on him after he retired). His teeth were now plugged with meat and he was picking at his teeth with his fingers.

Junior, Dwight's stepson, walked up to him with a determined look on his face. Price thought, "Uh, oh. Junior's got a beef and he's picked now, while we're trying to get outta here, to have it out with me."

Junior was a weight lifter and was built like a brick shit house. He was also an excellent soldier. He emulated his step father, Dwight, and wanted to be just like him. Junior was fast approaching, in rank, to doing just that.

"You need a toothpick?" Junior asked Colonel Price.

"Come again?"

"You need a toothpick? You're picking at your teeth with your fingers. Very unsanitary."

"You gotta toothpick? Out here on the tarmac?"

"Fuck'n-A." With that, Junior opened his wallet and pulled out a toothpick. "They're the plastic kind, with a brush," Junior added. "Easier on your gums. Got floss, too."

"Well, I'll be go to hell," Colonel Price sputtered, running a plastic toothpick through his teeth. "You are Dwight's son, I mean, stepson. That's something Mr. Think-of-Everthing, Dwight Jones, would have — toothpicks and floss in his wallet. I like these plastic toothpicks, by the way."

"Yep, that's who I copied it from, and thanks for comparing me to my step-pappy," smiled Junior. "He's a good man."

"Yes he is," agreed Price. "One hell of a man. If he's your model, you got the best."

"Thanks. I wanna be the best."

On the long flight home over the ocean, both Price and Junior, and an airplane full of soldiers, watched in disbelief and awe as Sergeant Jones single-handedly saved the Australian Jumbo Jet from what could have been a tragic fire and possible death to them all. There was a fire in the rear toilet, and Dwight, with his bare hands, ripped out an exhaust fan from the ceiling, for which he received severe burns on his hands.

Price made a mental note to present Sergeant Jones with a Challenge Coin when they arrived on the ground. There was already a surprise Bronze Star award for Dwight at the 451's return home ceremony in Erkson. Price could present the coin to Dwight then.

However, when the soldiers were disembarking the Jumbo Jet at Ft. Sill, Oklahoma, and many of them were kissing the tarmac, including Dwight, Price made the snap decision to present Dwight with the coin then and there.

Challenge Coins, also known as Impact Awards, were carried by Colonels and Sergeant Majors, and handed out surreptitiously to soldiers for a job well done. Soldiers cherished them, often more so than medals, like the Bronze Star.

Price walked up to Dwight as he was standing up from kissing the ground. Price held out his hand to shake. Dwight held up his bandaged right hand. They both looked at it and laughed. Instead of shaking hands, and passing the coin from palm to palm as was tradition, Price stuck the coin in Dwight's blouse pocket and walked away.

Tears shot from Dwight's eyes like a squirt gun. No words were exchanged. Many soldiers saw the presentation. A hush fell over the entire tarmac.

Colonel Price was terribly concerned about the high rate of suicides amongst the 451 soldiers upon their return from deployment. He didn't understand it. Out of a group of soldiers who had been involved in and witnessed certain horrific incidents, some appeared to be unfazed and quite normal, while others went off the deep end. Why? Were they mentally unbalanced to start with?

Price spent quite a bit of time investigating one suicide, talking to the family, trying to determine just what went wrong, and if he or the National Guard could have been more supportive. Given two men, about the same age, both Christian, both about the same amount of education, both coming home to divorce and bankruptcy—one takes his life, the other takes it in stride. What gives?

"It's all relevant," Price knew, "to the individual." He could understand the clash of worlds, of being so involved, of having so much responsibility, at the same time gunfire was going off, and rockets screamed over head, and IED's exploded. It's like a drug. Soldiers get addicted to the fear, and violence and, yes, even the guilt. And then they come home to stocking shelves at Casey's. Should the Twinkies go here beside the bread, or over in the candy section? For some it was a relief (no one was dying), and to others it was like a tectonic shift of brain lobes, one saying, "Is this all there is?" the other saying, "You might as well end it right now, right here in the aisle of Casey's." (That actually happened.)

The guilt was such a huge part—feeling responsible for something that happened, most notably someone getting killed. Dwight was a good example. In the Humvee rollover that killed Blankenship and Black (Price had trouble keeping the two straight), Dwight had helped recruit one, telling him the Guard only served state-side; the other Dwight had talked into transferring to the 451, where men where men. With Washington and Stein, Dwight had given them a route that was supposed to be safe, but it led into a trap. Poor Dwight felt responsible for four deaths, and countless more, considering all the convoys of other battalions he gave directions to. And Dwight was a top-notch soldier. Bert hoped he was alright. Whenever Bert asked Dwight how he was doing, it was always, "I'm fine, I'm fine." Bert knew otherwise. Reports were coming to him about Dwight's divorce and DUI and obesity. But how could he help if Dwight wasn't willing? There was such a Colonel-Sergeant wall there that Dwight seemed to have to maintain. Price would have liked to break down that wall and become just friends or pals with soldiers like Dwight, but it seemed near impossible.

Price himself was responsible for some deaths, he knew. He was responsible for all of them, actually, being in command. But there was Volger, who Price had ordered back in the field, only for him to die of dehydration. Jesus, if Price had known he was going to do something like that, he could have gotten rid of him as unfit. But they were short of men the way it was, and it took forever to get replacements. Decisions were made at the time that were correct given the circumstances. Circumstances changed. If he had known then what he knew now, would he have made a different decision? Probably. But that's hindsight.

And mistakes were made, yes. If Bert went around feeling guilty about every error he made, he would be in the crapper. No, he was not going down that rabbit hole. He knew he had done the very best he could. He never made a decision based on self interest, but on what he perceived to be the best interests of the 451. Sometimes he erred. He was human.

Then, not only were there the suicides and divorces, but also DUI's, drug overdoses, even robberies and murder. Jesus Christ! What the hell happened to the outstanding men he had seen stepping up to the plate in Iraq?

One hapless soul, after coming home to a divorce and finding out that his wife had used his money to buy her boyfriend a new Corvette, was caught up in a convenience store heist where a clerk was killed. A couple of other soldiers were homeless. One was living in his car. The other came around to Bert's house borrowing money. Bert always gave it to him, knowing it was going for drugs or liquor or both, and that he would never be paid back. He didn't care. The other he took food to in his car, appalled at how mentally deranged he was, with long greasy hair and dirty clothes. He had been one of the sharpest soldiers in the 451. Now look at him. Gone to Hell. Why these vets wouldn't check into the V.A., Bert somewhat understood. There were so many horror stories. But compared to the condition these soldiers were in now, the V.A., to Bert, looked pretty good.

Bert felt a certain responsibility to the men who had served under him. They were his family then, they were still his family. He hated to admit it, but the 451 might have been better off left in Iraq to fight to the duration.

But the duration was what, a total pullout of Afghanistan in 2021? It was just a total cluster fuck all the way around. No wonder some of his men felt like failures.

But Bert Price didn't. He had wanted to be in command of an engineering battalion, and he was proud of what they accomplished. But what did they accomplish? They had built a school (that was burned down by the Taliban). They had helped set up free elections (the people had no idea who they were voting for). They installed the Mother Of All Generators (that was constantly under attack and would eventually be destroyed). Was Iraq any better off after the 451 left? Price had to stop and think. To be honest, probably not. These one-year deployments of volunteer units, one after the other, wasn't accomplishing much, if anything. Their real mission was to keep their heads down and return home safe and sound. Trillions of dollars was being spent on a war that would never be won. That money could be used at home to provide day care, higher education, infrastructure, you-name-it.

Of Bert Price's 32 year career in the military, 19 of those years was spent with the 451 Engineering Battalion. After returning home from deployment in Iraq he was put in charge of General Distribution and Planning. It was a heady job, figuring out what all the troops would need and when, and then getting it to them when they were deployed. He remembered what it was like, not having armored vehicles. That would not happen on his watch.

He spent a couple of years in Kosovo as an adviser to NATO. He retired in 2018 at the age of 50. He could have landed a job most anywhere, but didn't even try. His kids had pretty much left home, and his wife and he didn't have the financial need they once had. His two sons both joined the National Guard and served in the Middle East. One of the sons wouldn't speak to him. Bert wasn't sure why. It might have something to do with politics. Bert is a die-hard Republican, where the son who won't speak to him, is a Democrat. Politics! Bert hated to see his family split over something they had no control over, but what could he do?

Price may be retired, but he's not letting grass grow under his feet. He's on many boards, committees and fund raising organizations, from church, to Scouts, to school boards and alumni associations. He is on the go full time. There is never any downtime for Bert Price.

He helped his interpreter in Iraq immigrate to the United States. He helps Kosovo refugees find a home in America. He assisted Grover in becoming a sister community to a community in Kosovo, and helps with immigration. He helped raise funds for Kosovo families who were victims of war.

If he had to do it all over again he probably wouldn't change much, except he might not be such a hard-ass. He had to step on some people to get where he did, and for that he has regrets. He lost some friends, that turned into enemies when he needed them. But he knows that is sort of the unwritten rule of the military: look out for yourself, and climb up anyone's back necessary to get where you want to go. He doesn't lose any sleep over his actions.

He's real proud of Kurt Dingman and wants nothing more than to see Kurt as a Brigadier General. Bert has made all the recommendations he could to that effect. Kurt Dingman and Dwight Jones' statistical analysis of IED locations was original and a game changer in the war against terrorism. It's just too bad that war was such a failure. The Taliban took over Afghanistan in what? 24 hours? After the U. S. had been in the Middle East 20 freaking years! Unreal.

Unlike many of the soldiers in the 451, Bert Price sleeps good at night. He doesn't have nightmares about people dying. He occasionally dreams about Volger with a bottle of water in his hand, or a black and yellow BMW buzzing around like a bumble bee. But it's quickly replaced by the Mother Of All Generators, traveling at a snail's pace across the desert, being shot at, but deflecting the bullets. It's a happy dream, and Bert wakes up feeling good, ready to take on the day.

Facebook "Friends"

Bert Price looked at the Facebook message. It was from Jerome Birdsil. Bert had requested Jerome to be a "Friend" on Facebook. (Bert liked to keep track of his military associates. He had over 2,000 "Friends.") Jerome had been his Staff Sergeant and right hand man, taking care of a lot of the nit-picky details of commanding a battalion and seeing to it that loose ends were tied up. Jerome kept Bert's schedule, reminding him of meetings, disciplinary procedures that needed attended to, and generally keeping things tidy for the Colonel. As a special assignment, Jerome proofed Bert's Newsletters that he sent to the families of the 451. Jerome wasn't especially good at grammar, but he was a good second eye—particularly after Bert stayed up all night working on a newsletter when he couldn't sleep. Bert gave him full rein to make any changes he thought necessary, which was both a blessing and problematic. It was Price's name that went on the Newsletter, when in fact, it was Jerome who sometimes wrote or rewrote a major section.

Bert had lost track of Jerome after they were stateside and discharged from the Guard, and was wondering what Jerome was up to. Jerome had always been a good guy, a person Bert could count on to carry out his instructions explicitly. The return Facebook message from Jerome caught Bert off guard.

"Fuck you, Price, you asshole! You're the last person on earth I want to be 'friends' with. If I ever see you walking down the street I will either cross over to the other side, or I will kick you in the nuts (if you have any), spit on you, and maybe even whip out my dick and piss on you. You fucked over so many people, including me, and now you want to be friends?!?! I would rather see you dead and in hell where you belong than to be a 'friend' of yours. Don't ever try to contact me again, because you are a nightmare in my life, one that I don't want to relive. I have worked hard to put cocksuckers like you in the past and move forward to a new life. I don't need you to fuck it up, again! So fuckoff, motherfucker! I hope I have made my self quite clear!"

Price stared at the message. "Indeed," he thought. "You have made yourself quite clear," and wondered if Jerome might by suffering from PTSD or depression or both, although Jerome was mainly involved with office work, not the actual removal of IED's where soldiers were killed. Jerome had friends who were killed, however. The new term that was being bandied about was "post secondary PTSD." And the rates of PTSD and depression were quite high in returning 451 soldiers—too high.

Price thought back to their time in Iraq. He always liked Jerome, and felt they got along well. He denied Jerome a promotion because he thought another soldier was more qualified. Jerome said he understood and was okay with the decision. Had he been lying?

Then there was the Purple Heart Jerome had requested. It was an odd story. In cities like Ramadi, streets, if you could call them streets, were crisscrossed with dangling telephone and electrical wires. If it was windy—and the hot, dry air was usually blowing in off the desert—the wires would get to swinging back-and-forth. To keep the wires from shorting, Iraqis weighted the wires down with hanging bags of whatever—sand, junk, even human waste. When the military vehicles moved through the streets, the low hanging bags were a nuisance, not to mention filthy. Soldiers moved the bags out of the way with long poles. As soldiers would often do, they got to batting the bags around, making a game out of it. Jerome, who had his blouse off against regulation, took a swing at one of the bags. It burst open and dumped its contents, which was human excrement, all over him, causing a type of chemical burn. He was treated for it and was fine. Sometime later he put in for a Purple Heart, claiming the burn was a combat related injury. Price was asked to verify. Price stated what he knew, which was a completely different story than Jerome told. He was denied the Purple Heart. Evidently Jerome held a grudge for that and possibly the lack of promotion.

Price took it all in stride (as long as his family wasn't threatened). Some officers he knew took a dressing down like that real personal. But Price knew better. He let it shed, like water off a duck's back. He knew he made his decisions based on the best information he had at the time, that he made mistakes (although he didn't feel he had in this case) and made enemies. In fact, Price wouldn't have risen to the position he had in the military, a Full Bird Colonel, without stepping on some people, or climbing up their backs. It was the way the military operated. You had to be willing to fuck your buddy over to get where you wanted. It was a sign, according to the military, of good leadership—the ability to make hard-nosed decisions and live with the consequences. Those who couldn't were limited in how far they could go. Major battlefield decisions were made in split seconds. Sometimes they were wrong, and cost lives. But it was the overall objective that was important. Price thought about the blunders military leaders such as Grant and Patton and even Washington had made that cost thousands of lives. But look at what they accomplished.

Price would not block Jerome from contacting him. Maybe someday Jerome would need help (he might need help now) and Bert would be able to provide it. Price helped a lot of people with disability, counseling, even Gulf War Syndrome, which he thought was pure bullshit.

Jerome might be pissed now, but who knew what the future would hold?

Four DUI's

It was after his fourth DUI, and the judge's threat of prison time as an habitual offender, that Scot Victor decided to get help. He hated waking up, or coming to, in a jail cell, not remembering how he got there, and having to call his parents, or his brother, or his on-again off-again girlfriend, or a drinking buddy to come bail him out. Actually, he lied to the judge and told her that he knew he had a drinking problem and that he was getting help from the VA. (He was trying to get a reduced sentence.) It worked, but the judge, being wise, insisted on verification, so Scot had to follow through and call the VA.

The VA gave him medications and told him to come back in two weeks if it wasn't working. It wasn't, so they gave him other, stronger medications, which didn't work either. Scot was having thoughts of killing himself. The only way he could think of doing it was to go out in the barn on his parents' farm and hang himself. In a weak moment, he mentioned those thoughts to the VA and he wound up in in-patient treatment.

It was in counseling that he learned he was trying to self-medicate with alcohol (it is a pain killer) and, let's be honest, drugs, especially meth. Meth made him feel so good that he forgot all about what he went through in Iraq; or it made him so paranoid he wanted to curl up in a ball and shiver and shake and cry. He never knew which it was going to be.

He had a "friend" who had a portable cooking unit that he operated out of his car while driving around and selling. Everything was fine and dandy until the portable cooking unit blew up in his "friend's" lap. It could not be determined if the "friend" died from the explosion or the car fire that resulted from the explosion. The whole event was an eye-opening experience for Scot and he knew he had to make some major life changes. Ya think?

His on-again off-again girlfriend informed him she was pregnant, which added to his stress. He couldn't see himself as a father. Why would anyone want to bring a child into this world? His on-again off-again, being of sounder mind, wouldn't even consider an abortion.

The National Guard had promised tuition assistance so he tried studying to become an Industrial Arts teacher at the Community College in Grover. When he came to class drunk and almost cut off his finger in a table saw, the Community College advised they no longer wanted him as a student.

So, he tried HVAC at the Community College in Rochester. He was bound and determined he was going to get that tuition money out of the government. After all, it was the main reason he signed up for the National Guard. But he was too depressed to go to class, and couldn't get over his "friend" dying in the meth explosion. Shit, all those IED deaths in Iraq, and then he comes home to another one. Life sucked, war sucked, and Scot Victor wanted to die.

In his dreams he saw a little girl's body lying on the sand, or a chopped off hand on a pile of explosives, or beheaded Iraqis. Very seldom were his dreams not nightmares. He was afraid to go to sleep. His brother tried to talk to him. His parents tried to talk to him. His father, a Vietnam Veteran, said, "Buck up son. At least you didn't have garbage thrown at you when you came home."

"But why were we there, Dad? This is a war without end. The Iraqis don't want us there. The only thing we're doing is protecting our own troops. The insurgents are as strong as ever, maybe stronger. The U.S. being there is the greatest recruitment tool they have. Their only wish is to die fighting us and becoming a martyr. They call us the infidels. What are we doing there?"

Scot's dad shrugged his beefy shoulders. "My country calls, I go. End of story."

"That's a copout, Dad."

"Copout? I'll tell you what's a copout, son. It's you, no job, drinking and drugging—don't deny it—yourself to death, and your girlfriend pregnant. Be a man. Make an honest woman out of her. Take responsibility."

The best help Scot received was through group sessions in either the VA or AA. He was surprised and even a little disappointed to find out that he was not unique. Other veterans had almost the identical feelings he had. They wanted to die. They had seen too much killing and felt responsible for it. Why were they alive and others dead? What was the country's purpose for being in the Middle East? Why did the U.S. send troops into war so poorly equipped?

That was one of Scot's biggest beefs. He couldn't believe they were sent to fight a war with equipment not up to the task. Then, when the 451 upgraded their own equipment, it caused more deaths. It was a Catch 22. Other battalions returned or were returning with no casualties. Four of the 451's soldiers were killed and others severely injured. One of the dead soldiers didn't even belong to the 451. He was just riding along. Was the 451 a jinx?

It didn't make any sense to spend a year there and then get the hell out. It was like dipping your toes in the water and saying you went in for a swim. Scot, remembering his fullback days ("Just kick ass, Victor!) was always taught that you fight to win, not just show up and say you were there.

As it turned out, the only job Scot could hold onto for any length of time was housekeeping at the VA (night janitor). It was a brainless job, but it kept him close to the VA counselors and group sessions. He knew, without a doubt, that if he hadn't gone into the National Guard he would have followed in his brother's footsteps and made something of himself. Why at 17, he thought he wanted to go into the National Guard, he has no idea. Part of it was to not follow the same path as his brother, and the other part was to piss off his parents. It was a dumb move on his part and he was paying for it now. The recruiter had lied and promised that the National Guard stayed home.

Scot now has a little girl that he has custody of three days a week. He does love the little girl, and is glad that his ex and he didn't go through with an abortion. Little girls have more of a chance of success in the world, he believes. They aren't near as apt to run off in the military as men. Some of them do. It's just that odds are more in favor of little girls using common sense.

In 2021 Scot watched in shocked disbelief as the United States military pulled out of Afghanistan. Afghans rioted trying to escape the country. Scot got so drunk he forgot it was his day to pick up his little girl. His ex filed an injunction barring him from seeing his little girl, saying he was alcoholic and suicidal.

Scot's life is in his hands. He has no idea what he's going to do with it. Thank you National Guard.

Gluten Free

Going on 15 years after he served with the 451 in Iraq, Chaplain Joe Fordice still makes sure all the windows and doors of his house are closed and locked before he goes to bed. He knows all too well what lurks in the night. He would rather shut out the cool night air, and let the house get stuffy, than run the risk of "the enemy" getting in.

Occasionally, although not as often, he still sees the faces of dead soldiers in his dreams and wakes up screaming. His wife holds him until it passes, until he realizes he is home and safe, and not in Iraq. But he can smell it, and taste it.

When he first came back from Iraq, and his wife was driving, he would constantly tell her she was way too close to the vehicle in front of her, even though she was not tail-gating at all. Convoys in Iraq were required to maintain 50 meters distance between vehicles, in case one was hit by an IED or RPG, it wouldn't take down the vehicle in front or behind it. Manhole covers drove him nuts.

Fourth-of-July fireworks were real hard on him, and he was a non-combat, non-weapon carrying Chaplain. He took care of people, he didn't fight. It was all the overhead rockets, all the dead and injured people he cared for, all of the confessions he heard from soldiers who wanted nothing more than to stay alive and go home safely, that made him jumpy.

The knuckles of his right hand are constantly swollen and painful. He's not sure why, but he feels it is tied to his service in Iraq. Eating gluten free helps some. He hates to admit he's superstitious — it's unbecoming of a clergyman — but he baptized with his right hand. It was his right hand he put in the water, then placed on the soldier's head, like the hand had committed a sin. A number of soldiers requested baptism, or rebaptism, especially before a dangerous mission. It was one of the good things he did while there. And a few soldiers came to accept Jesus Christ as their savior. Chaplain Fordice feels good about that.

He made a big mistake when he came home. He took no time off, or very little, and went right to work as a full-time Chaplain for the National Guard. That meant he was called upon to visit families of all the suicides that were taking place with returning soldiers — not just with the National Guard, but the full time Army, Marines, Navy and Air Force. There were even suicides with soldiers who had never been in combat or stationed in a combat zone. What the Hell was going on?

It was the stress of the suicides that pushed Chaplain Joe Fordice over the edge. He woke up every morning wanting to die and was contemplating suicide. Since his right hand was swollen up, he would slash the wrist of that hand. That would relieve the pressure and fix it.

A soldier had killed himself one week, and Chaplain Fordice visited the family. Then there was another suicide the next week. The base Commander called and said, "You have to stop this. These suicides are giving us a bad name."

Fordice came unglued. "Do something? I didn't send them to Iraq! You think I'm God? I can't do this anymore. Take me out!" That's when psychiatry visited with him and he was given a medical discharge. Colonel Price was asked to substantiate the conditions that Chaplain Joe Fordice was exposed to. Colonel Price was glad to assist and was instrumental in Chaplain Fordice receiving disability. Fordice hated to accept it, but other soldiers were receiving disability for less severe disorders.

Chaplain Joe Fordice now drives a school bus. The screaming kids are actually less stressful than the military, and the kids' loud voices are somewhat of a comfort compared to gunfire.

Does he regret his service in Iraq? Yes he does. It was terribly hard on his family. He had three small kids at the time — there were birthdays missed, and he didn't get to help teach his daughter to fish or ride a bike. It was terribly hard on him.

The worst part, however, is that he doesn't believe the US Military accomplished anything of benefit in the Middle East — especially with the recent pullout of troops from Afghanistan. It was twenty years of non-stop war that accomplished absolutely nothing.

And that may be the reason for all of the suicides, including what was almost his own. The war in the Middle East, like the war in Vietnam (which resulted in a lot of suicides also, i.e. more veterans died of suicide following the war than were killed in the war) was a total failure all the way around, which equates to failure of the soldier. "Why go on living if the world is a failure and I'm a failure?"

There was also the issue of decompression. When World War II was over, it took the returning soldiers up to two months to get home by ship. It gave them ample time to talk amongst themselves and clear their head. Now, soldiers were in a war zone one day, and home 48 hours later, with little time to decompress. No wonder some of them went off the deep end.

Fordice is also curious as to why some soldiers seemed to handle the stress better than others. He looks at Price and Dingman as examples. They seemed to go on with their lives without much of a hitch after their return. Both Price and Dingman were officers, and had quite a bit of education. Fordice wonders if education is a factor — the higher the education, the better the individual handles stress? However, Fordice himself was highly educated and look at the mess he was in.

Fordice wouldn't have wanted to go to war with any other group of soldiers; they were all excellent men and women. But did they make the world a better place to live, like the soldiers in World War II? No.

And that's the fault of politics. But all wars are fraught with politics, Chaplain Fordice reasons. Truman didn't let Patton invade Russia, or MacArthur finish off Korea. George H.W. Bush pulled out of Iraq so his son, George W., could go back in. That was it. That was the reason for Iraq. It got George W. re-elected — wag the dog — and people killed, and lives destroyed, all for a man's ego. Soldiers fight and die while politicians get re-elected.

Hurt People Hurt People

Fourteen years after her deployment in Iraq, Chris Mitchel sat in a hot tub in the basement of their home and wanted to kill herself. It had been a hard day at work with the ambulance company. When she wasn't busy with the ambulance, she helped out in the ER checking people in and doing paper work. A Gulf War Veteran came in demanding treatment, saying he was a veteran on full disability, that he received $5,000 a month, and he had a brand new Dodge Ram pick-up in the parking lot. He demanded pain killers. Chris, of course, had a soft spot for veterans, but not veterans making demands. Why he had to mention his new Dodge Ram pick-up and $5,000 a month disability, she had no idea. What did that have to do with anything? Was he trying to impress someone? She listened to just so much of his huffing and blowing, asked if he was high on pain killers already, and told him if he didn't quiet down she would call the police (which would be her husband) and have him checked for simulated intoxication. When the veteran started to object, she reached for the phone, and he bolted. She watched through the window as he got in his big, new Dodge Ram (it was red, he hadn't mentioned that it was red) and sped off, pulling out in front of a car on the highway and nearly causing an accident. She should have called the police then, but let it slide. Hopefully he wouldn't kill someone. He was a vet.

Chris, a veteran herself, couldn't tolerate other veterans taking advantage of their military service, and lording it over people, like the world owed them a living. Most of the veterans she had served with had had the shit kicked out of them, were quiet, and wanted nothing more than to just be left alone. Many of them, herself included, had benefits coming they didn't even use, or want to use. Where this blow-hard joker came from, she had no idea, but it riled her to the core. Once riled, she had a hard time letting go of things she had no control over—something she knew she needed to work on—which ultimately led to, "I'm no good, I never have been, I might as well kill myself."

When she had gotten home from work, and the kids climbed all over her, which she was grateful for, she pushed them aside and said, "Mommy needs a little time out. Give me twenty minutes in the hot tub. Okay?"

She had homemade wine in the basement which she made herself. She poured herself a large tumbler full, eased herself into the hot water, and laid her head back. It felt good, and the wine and hot water went straight to her head. She saw a vision of Herman Stein asking if this was gonna be the day he got his Purple Heart.

"Mommy, do you want another glass of wine?"

It was her little girl. The twenty minutes were up, in fact it had been an hour, and her little girl was there. Instead of her little girl asking her to climb out of the hot tub and play with them, her little girl was asking if she wanted another glass of wine. Chris almost said yes. However, she caught herself. Her dad had been an alcoholic, and she had made a vow it would never happen to her, although she knew she had it in her genes.

"Hand me my bathrobe, Hon," she said, and almost fell over reaching for it.

It was then she knew she needed help.

It had been fourteen years of saying, "No, no, I'm alright. I don't need help." Which really meant she did need help. But Chris wasn't going to ask the VA. She had hauled too many veterans to the VA in an ambulance. She had seen how the VA handled, abused (yes, abused), and misdiagnosed veterans. She would have nothing to do with the VA.

Chris would form her own self-help group.

She decided to go to a 451 reunion at Herman Stein's mother's house and recruit some members. Herman's mother held a "Herman Stein Reunion" once a year to get the soldiers to come and reminisce about Iraq and tell stories about Herman the jokester, the sand angel maker, the impersonator.

A further tragedy of Herman's death was that his little brother killed himself. He worshiped Herman and felt so bad about him dying, he stepped out in front of a semi. They were the only two boys in the family. Needless to say, Herman's mother was devastated and half crazy. Maybe full crazy.

Chris met Herman's daughter, Angie, whom Chris had promised she would tell all about her dad. Angie, now in her late teens, had tattoos and piercings all over her body. It was obvious she was a heavy drug user. When Chris tried to talk to her about Herman, Angie put out a hand to stop her. "Did he tell you he beat my mom?" she asked.

Chris said no more.

It was debatable if the reunions helped Herman's mother much, because they turned into drunk fests. And Chris drank right along with the rest of them. Herman was a Grain Belt drinker, so cases and kegs of GB were ordered up and consumed, and puked up. Chris thought Grain Belt was awful tasting stuff, but drank anyway to be part of the crowd.

Hurt people hurt people.

Chris overheard a drunken conversation. "You threw that flash-bang that killed that pregnant woman."

"What?"

"You heard me, Johnson. You threw that flash-bang."

"Well, yeah. What the hell was I s'posed to do? That crowd was closing in on us."

"How about firing your weapon in the air? Da."

"Well, fuck you!"

"Stop it!" screamed Chris. "We're supposed to be here having a good time and helping Herman's mother. Not ragging on each other."

"Who made you God almighty, Mitchel? You let Herman die. Did you tell his daughter that?"

Chris was stunned. Her mouth dropped open but no words came out. How could anyone say such a thing? She turned on her heel, left the "pity party," never to return to another Herman Stein Reunion. The hurt caused by those words was overwhelming. How anyone could think or say that she could have saved Herman's life, and didn't, was just trying to hurt her, trying to cover up their own guilt feelings for what they did in Iraq. Herman was burned to a crisp. In civilian EMS they were called "crispy critters" by firemen. In the military, they were called "smokies"--"little smokies" for kids, "big smokies" for adults. Herman was a "big smokie" and no one could have saved him except God. And God didn't.

Hurt people hurt people.

She put a tiny ad in the local newspaper. "Self Help Reboot Group Forming, Warriors With Wings, for Veterans or Anyone Suffering From PTSD. Will meet in the basement of the Methodist church, 801 Locust St., Sunday night at 8:00 p.m."

Chris sat there for a full hour and no one showed up. She was about to leave when she heard the side door creak open. There was a thin man standing in the door with sunken eyes. "Am I in the right place?" he asked.

"You're in the right place."

His name was Harry. He wasn't a veteran. He had been involved in a drunken car accident that killed the driver of another car, a woman who was a wife and a mother. He was waiting trial for vehicular homicide, manslaughter, or possibly even murder. He wasn't sure. The state hadn't decided. Harry felt terrible and wanted to die. He wasn't to the point of admitting he had a drinking problem, however. He just knew that on that fateful fatal night, he drank too much, crossed the center line and killed someone. The worst part was that he saw the woman crushed in the car before the police cuffed and led him away. The air bags had deployed, but the engine of the little foreign car had come in on top of her.

"You're killing yourself won't bring that woman back," Chris told him.

"I know. But it will sure the hell get me off this planet."

"You have a wounded soul, Harry," she told him. "Let's look at healing your soul."

"My soul? My soul is evil."

"No, no. Think of your soul as maybe like your heart. If the heart is diseased, or punctured, what can we do to heal it? There's surgery, medication, therapy, counseling."

"You know?" Harry said. "I sorta feel better already. I gotta heal my soul. You're right, it hurts right here in my chest, where my heart is."

"That's great. We can't do anything about your trial coming up. But we can do something about today."

Where Chris got her counseling ability, she had no idea. It just came to her naturally, and people opened up to her. She had no idea if she was hurting or helping Harry.

The door creaked open again. Chris just about fell out of her chair. It was the blow-hard veteran who had been demanding pain killers at ER.

Pete didn't remember Chris. Which was a good thing. Pete was an original Gulf War Veteran who had served, not particularly fought (he was in supply), under Storm'n Norman Schwarzkopf. His "disability," if you could call it a disability was, he had, or said he had, Gulf War Syndrome, a condition related to the hot, arid conditions of the Persian Gulf. Somehow, he had managed to convince the VA that he was deserving of full disability. He was obviously a con artist.

After several meetings with Wounded Warriors he admitted that he told people he was wounded in combat in the Gulf War.

"Why is it important for you to tell people you were wounded when you weren't?" Chris asked.

Pete leaned forward with his face in his hands. "I want people to feel sorry for me, I guess. It's an ego thing, I 'spose." He swallowed hard, his Adam's Apple bobbing up and down. "I've never said this before to anyone."

Remembering her experience with Pete at the ER, Chris wanted to go on the attack, but checked herself. Wounded Warriors was supposed to "reboot" people, not crush them. "Do you know what ego is an acronym for?" she asked.

"What?"

"Edge God Out."

"I don't believe in God."

"Do you believe in a higher power?"

"Oh, yeah."

"What is your Higher Power, Pete?"

"Percodan, Darvon, Fentanyl."

Chris thought, "Oh, Jesus Christ," but didn't say anything. At least Pete was talking, and being honest, and not keeping his feelings buried under his shell of bullshit. "What would happen if you didn't have the pain meds, Pete?"

"I would be in Hell. I'd kill myself."

"How would you kill yourself?"

"Oh, I dunno. Gun in my mouth, gun to my head, hang myself."

"Do you hear voices, Pete? Is that why you want to destroy your head?"

"Yes."

"What are the voices telling you, Pete?"

"To get the hell out of here. Run!"

"Are you afraid to patch up that soul?"

"Yes."

"What's really causing your soul sickness, Pete?"

"My dad molested me as a boy. I've never told anyone before."

"Maybe you should confront your dad."

"He's dead."

"Maybe you should forgive him."

"Forgive him? I'd like to kill the sonofabitch, if I could."

"Why did he molest you, Pete?"

"Why? He, he..."

"He what, Pete?"

"He needed to get off. He, he, he was molested by his brothers when he was a little boy." Pete slumped down in his chair, exhausted, like a wet rag.

"Could you write your dad a letter?"

"I don't wanna."

"Why don't you wanna write him a letter, Pete?"

"Because, because..."

"Because why, Pete? Does this hurt your comfort zone? Do you not want to heal your soul and go on hurting?"

"This is all too confusing. Leave me the fuck alone."

And so it went. Pete and Chris actually became friends and confidants.

Harry was given a deferred sentence on the condition he attend AA. He did and admitted he was an alcoholic. He worked the 12 Steps with a sponsor and made amends to the family of the woman he killed. They forgave him. It was a miracle of recovery.

The group grew. Pete helped chair Wounded Warrior meetings. He was actually a good listener when not hyped up on pain meds, which he quit using. Another group was formed. Some of the 451 soldiers attended and talked about what happened. Herman Stein's name came up of course. The general consensus was that he was asking for it, he wanted to die. Chris held her breath, but there was no blame-gaming. John Washington was talked about, how he wasn't even with the 451, but was killed trying to help them out while on his way home. Arnold Allen Schwarzendruber's name came up a lot, and the little hole in his throat. Black and Blankenship came up and it was debated if they were killed by an IED or Humvee rollover, or both. Eddie Beams was cried over. Dwight Jones even showed up and talked about how his computer analysis both saved and killed people.

A woman dropped in, one of the few women to do so. She sat in a corner, looked at the floor and didn't say much. She said she just wanted to listen. It was Candice Beams, Eddie Beams' wife. Eddie had already been talked about, so his name didn't come up when she was there.

Finally Candice said, or asked, "How do you let go?"

There was silence in the group. Chris looked at Pete and motioned with her head for him to take it.

"What do you want to let go of?" he asked Candice?

"My husband," she whispered, and continued to stare at the floor.

Pete was about to say something, when she added, "The National Guard. The VA. The government. People who judge."

"That's a lot to let go of," Pete commented, not knowing what he was going to say next. He just gave it a shot. "Let's take them one at a time. "Your husband..."

Dwight Jones was in the group. He had just realized who the lady was. "Your husband is Eddie Beams."

"Yes," she whispered.

Dwight's mind flashed to the funeral where he had come apart and Candice had helped him. "Can you wave good-bye?" he asked.

"What do you mean?" she asked.

All-in-all a lot of burden was relieved, and healing accomplished by the Wounded Warriors that Chris Mitchel started.

Hurt people hurt people.

An artist painted wings on the side of a downtown building where the second meeting was held. When a person "graduated" from the program, they stood in front of the wings and had their picture taken. Warriors with Wings.

Chris' husband, Jocko, even attended and talked about some of the gruesome incidents he had been involved in. He had killed a person in the line of duty as a police officer, and admitted that he wouldn't have had to shoot the person, but did anyway because he wanted to. It was ruled a justifiable police shooting. He even talked about his feelings when Chris was deployed. He talked about his frustrations with her now. He wanted the old Chris back. She told him the old Chris had moved on, and that he had to, too. He understood. Their marriage grew stronger.

Chris is not one to sit around and brew in her own stew. She has put Iraq behind her, but not forgotten it. She is more concerned about the challenges and opportunities of each new day. She has hope. There is a great life ahead for her and her family, and she intends to have it, to live it. One day at a time. One second at a time.

One of Chris' Facebook Posts: There is a lot of work still to be done but I can honestly say there is no going backwards to the dark places I have been. There is only now and life is too short. That being said...not only will I fight for myself I will fight along beside you when you vote with your own feet to fight back. Love you All!!

She is a beautiful
piece of broken
pottery, put back
together by her
own hands. And a
critical world judges
her cracks
while missing the
beauty of how she
made herself
whole again.

J.M. Storm

Candice Beams "liked" the post with a "heart" and commented, "You go girl!"

Attitude Is a Form of Capital

Whenever he can, Kurt Dingman grabs his fly rod and heads for Decorah, Iowa for a little trout fishing and quiet time. He's preparing his dissertation for a PhD. There's a quaint motel on the Upper Iowa River where he likes to stay one, two, even three nights. He might get up early, work on the dissertation until mid-afternoon, then grab the fly rod and see what he can tease onto his mayfly or lightning bug, depending on what's buzzing around the water. Or he might fish early, then work in the afternoon. He always releases what he catches, mostly brook trout or an occasional walleye, no matter how big or small. He loves the color of the brookies, and holds them in his hand, letting the light reflect off their orange belly, and marvels at how the white speckles on their back blend in with the orange on their fins. He always dips his hand into the chilly water first before handling a fish so he doesn't contaminate their skin with the oil on his.

Most of the trout are hatchery raised now, he knows, and released into the water of the Driftless Area, so called because it was never covered by ice during the last Ice Age. (Sort of drifty, like he is. He teases his mind with the analogy.) Kurt laments that the trout are hatchery raised, rather than wild, and on their own. The hatchery-raised trout aren't as bright, and don't put up near the fight as the wild ones. Sometimes he can tell by the scars on their lips, that they have been caught two and three times. If the world were more like trout, he thinks, life would be easier, with less mayhem and bloodshed. But that would be the ideal world. From his studies of management, military science, and experience, he knows that attitude is a form of capital.

He is in line for promotion to General in the National Guard, which would be a one star, or Brigadier General. He has no idea whether he will make it or not, but having a PhD would be a big plus. Competition is stiff and he knows that frivolous factors often come into play. Timing and need are critical. His record is stellar: promoted to Full Colonel, in command of the 451, responsible for devising a statistical method in Iraq for finding IED's; cool under fire. The story of his hunting down a bomb-making insurgent in Iraq is legendary. Although Dingman killing the insurgent, when the insurgent had surrendered, or attempted to surrender, can either work against or for him, depending on the whim of the board. Some see it as justice, others criminal.

Kurt grabs his fly rod and heads out after a morning of study. The waters of the Upper Iowa are dark and cold, the sky overcast. Perfect for trout fishing. If it's too sunny at this time of day, the trout become lazy and rest. If it's too cold, the insects won't be buzzing, attracting trout. There's very little breeze, ideal for fly casting.

He casts long and high, aiming for the calm water along the opposite bank. The fly lands perfectly and settles in to float along down stream. In front of a little brush pile, the water explodes, and a nice brook grabs the lady bug and takes it into deeper water of midstream. Kurt's heart thumps. He saw the sun sparkle off its belly. It's good size. He plays out line, and lets it run, letting it think it has free ride, before he starts to slowly draw it in. Kurt has to be careful. He is using light test, and doesn't want to lose this one. He will have to wear this big boy down slowly.

It takes 45 minutes of painstaking work to draw the played out trout near enough to net. It's a beauty — 16 inches and over four pounds. His heart skips a beat. After dipping his hand in water, Kurt holds the wriggling fish up to the light. He wasn't sure, but now he is. This is no hatchery brook. It's a wild one.

Kurt can tell from its bright colors, and ugly features, and scars on its face and head. He's a fighter, the real thing. It seems to speak to him, "Take me."

Kurt wants to keep it badly. He could eat this one, take the wildness into himself, or even have it mounted. No one will know. There isn't another person in sight.

A vision of the scraggly insurgent, with his hands up, comes into his head. "Plez." Kurt's trigger finger tingles—the finger holding the brook by its gill. Kurt can see the "Release!" sign on the far bank, the face of the insurgent. He slips the brook into his creel and skedaddles back to the motel before anyone sees him. He has a little barbecue grill. He will grill this one, take in the wildness, and work on his dissertation.

Kurt struggled some with PTSD for the first few years after Iraq. He had migraine headaches and high blood pressure. He was taking 20 – 30 aspirin a day, chewing them without water. The lava-like grit reminding him of sand. He didn't know what was wrong but had suspicions. He Googled PTSD, and knew he had all the signs. Check check check. It helped just knowing what he had. Giving it a name weakened it. He would not get help. Why? He didn't know. Pride? Not wanting to admit he had a weakness? Was it a weakness? He had self diagnosed, he would self treat. Go easy on the liquor. Talk about it with some of his buddies who had been there. "Do loud noises bother you?" "Yeah, yeah." "Are you short of temper?" "Yeah, yeah." "Do you have thoughts of suicide?" (Tough question.) "Yeah, but I had those before Iraq. Doesn't everybody?" "I think so."

He tried to talk to Dwight. Dwight wouldn't talk. "I'm fine, I'm fine."

Bullshit.

The Pentagon flew Kurt and Dwight all over the country

training soldiers on their way over the pond, how to gather data, do the statistical analysis. Kurt's company flew him all over the world to train-the-trainer on Six Sigma. One time in a hotel meeting room, Kurt was heavy into a lecture. On the other side of the partition was a kitchen. Someone thumped a cooler door shut. Kurt hit the floor, everyone looking at him like maybe he'd had a heart attack. He called a quick break, but it would be days before his heartbeat returned to normal. He knew he should get help. Why was he so resistant? He didn't want it on his record, that was it. It could interfere with his chances for General.

Was it worth his health, his peace of mind? Yeah, to be a General was worth it.

Anyone who ever saw Kurt Dingman thought he looked like the All-American boy: clean cut, good looking, never-do-wrong, Kurt. They couldn't see his insides, which were churning — hate, guilt, fear — he had it all, a whirlwind of emotions.

He ran the Chicago Marathon with a full pack, just to prove he could do it. 26.2 miles of hell, well, the last 13.1 miles were. The hamstrings on the back of his right leg turned black-and-blue-and-red, and he wore a blister the size of a saucer into his left shoulder, from the backpack. He could hardly walk for three days, especially going down stairs at home, where no one could see him except his family. He had to go down steps backwards. But by golly he had done it, just to prove to himself he was one tough son-of-a-bitch. Or stupid? He wasn't sure. It was done. He had done it. No looking back. Move forward. Except it hurt. Accept the hurt, as a reward, badge of courage, like warriors of old.

"Honey, why do you do this to yourself?" his wife asked.

"Got to stay in shape."

"Stay in shape for what?"

"In case we're deployed again."

"You get deployed again, you can find yourself another wife."

"Oh, honey. Don't say that."

"I mean it. Let someone else fight that stupid war. Stupid, stupid, stupid."

Kurt knew she was right. But he was hooked — hook, line and sinker. Like that brook trout — a wild trout. Kurt wasn't hatchery raised.

He went before his dissertation panel. "Positive methods of motivation." Kurt spoke with authority, like he understood what he was talking about. He didn't, but he could see his thesis chair nodding his head in agreement, encouraging him. "There are three forms of motivation." It didn't matter whether he listed them or not. At that moment he couldn't remember the three, but he pushed on like a freight train through the night. "Positive psychological capitalism."

"What are the three forms of capital?" one of the old professors asked, mainly so that he could feel like he had asked a meaningful question.

Kurt didn't hesitate. "There is social capital." Kurt thought of Price who had a large network of people, and used them. "Organization is brands." Kurt didn't know what that meant, and he suspected his panel didn't either. It didn't matter. It was all an act anyway. "Financial capital — assets, cash on hand, borrowing power." Kurt could see eyes glazing over, so he hit them with the big one. "Attitude is a form capital." Their eyes lit up. They were paying attention. "If employees have certain characteristics within their organization, and it's positive, reflected down by management, it's more powerful than financial, and money is all powerful." The four member panel—three men and one woman—were beaming. He had pushed their button. "Optimism, resiliency, and competence, with equal self-efficacy (again, he didn't know what this meant, but he had memorized it in his fishing cabin), combine in a way to create, re-create, positive capital. Traits are inherited, states are created for organizational outcome, absolutely, but mostly for the good of the people."

Kurt passed his dissertation with flying colors, like a caddis fly nymph cast on air waves to the opposite shore. He was a Doctor of Philosophy, on his way, hopefully, to a one-star general, a Brigadier General in the Iowa National Guard. The PhD would help. Price might be comfortable with a master's degree and retiring as a Full Bird Colonel, but not Kurt Dingman. He wanted to be General Dingman, and take his place in history, when the next war came.

If there was a history.

Hell-of-a-Dog

Chaplain Joe Fordice was asked to perform the funeral service for Sergeant Eddie Beams by his wife Candice. Candice didn't know Chaplain Fordice personally, but Eddie had spoken highly of him, and said that Fordice was a good military Chaplain who did not judge people for believing something different than Christianity, or for having no belief at all, as in atheism. That was good enough for Candice. Eddie was half Native American (although she couldn't remember what Tribe, Eddie was vague about that, it was a combination of a couple) and believed more in a Great Spirit of the Universe rather than God and Jesus Christ. However, in a type of contradiction, Eddie told Candice that Jesus Christ had visited the Native Tribes after His death and resurrection, and taught them their ways. So why Eddie didn't believe in Jesus Christ, Candice didn't know, and didn't care. Chaplain Fordice had agreed to do the funeral, and that was all she wanted.

Chaplain Fordice was just relieved that Eddie's death was not by suicide like so many other soldiers' deaths he had been involved with. It stumped Fordice. Here Eddie Beams had been severely injured in Iraq, had PTSD up the yin-yang, was terribly disabled, yet he fought to stay alive. Others returning from Iraq had PTSD also, but were not physically disabled and could have made something of themselves, yet they took their own lives. Fordice could identify, having been close to suicide himself. Where was God in all this? The chatter was firing up again.

"Native Americans believed there were Minor Spirits," Chaplain Fordice explained to the people present at Eddie's funeral, "for the Sun and Moon and Water. Woman was created first, and when She conceived, She brought forth Man. The Soul is immortal and when it departs the body, according to the work it has done, it either joins the Gods in perpetual bliss or goes to the Sunset where it burns continually — a belief not that far removed from Christianity."

Fordice paused and studied the group of people assembled for the funeral. It was a large gathering, to honor a fallen hero. (Was Beams a hero? Fordice wondered. He had been elevated to that status because of his death.) There was a good mixture of civilians and military type people, some in uniform. Fordice went on, "I understand that, following the rocket attack that took the top of Eddie's head off, he met his ancestors several times, and was sent back to fulfill his work on Earth. Sergeant Edward Beams was a good man, and never surrendered his belief in country, family or mission. I believe he is now in that perpetual bliss he believed in. God bless America."

Dwight bit his bottom lip at the first volley of the 21-gun salute. This was no American Legion Honor Guard (old men with ancient weapons that parts fell off of every time they shot), this was the real thing from the 451 Combat Engineering Battalion of NE Iowa. They were active duty soldiers, using the latest rifles and blank ammunition. They looked sharp — white gloves, pressed uniform, shoes shined to such a sheen they looked like mirrors. The Commander barked orders, "Ready, Aim, Fire!"

Dwight jumped, even though he was ready.

He looked over at Candice Beams. She was dressed in black, complete with black gloves, black silk stockings, hat and veil. She never looked up. She just sat slumped forward, with her head down and her black-gloved hands folded in her lap. She had been through a lot, caring for her disabled husband after his return home.

When the triangular-folded American Flag was presented to her by the Commander on one knee, the flag in his outstretched, white-gloved hand, she still couldn't move or look up. Her son, who was sitting beside her, reached over and accepted the flag.

When taps were played, not on a prerecorded tape, but by an actual military bugle player, it was just too much. Dwight wailed uncontrollably, his fist either jammed in his mouth or his hands covering his face. Brandy, his wife, tried to comfort him. He was breathing so hard, he was gasping for breath.

"Someone help, please!" Brandy shouted. "He's having a panic attack."

Candice Beams moved off her seat and confronted Dwight, grabbing him by the jacket front. "It's alright, Dwight! He's in a better place!" she shouted. "He's with his ancestors!"

"They don't understand!" Dwight shouted back, looking at the crowd, and waving a hand at them. "They don't know what it was like! They weren't there!"

"They don't have to know, Dwight. All they need to know is that they're safe at night."

Dwight had had nothing to do with Sergeant Eddie Beams' death. It was the emotion of the 21-gun salute, and the bugle Taps that brought back so many memories of the others who were killed, ones that Dwight was responsible for.

Retired Colonel Price and now Brigadier General Kurt Dingman and others, including Major Dobbs, rushed forward and surrounded Dwight. It did little good. Dwight was close to passing out.

"Does any one have smelling salts?" Brandy hollered.

Major Dobbs got right in Dwight's face and slapped him.

"Dwight!" he shouted. "Dwight! I know now it wasn't your fault. I was wrong for blaming you. We were all doing the best we could with what we had. I'm the one who followed that wire, not you. It wasn't your fault. I forgive you."

"You do?" Dwight was suddenly alert and in control of himself. "You forgive me?"

"Of course I do, Dwight. I should have told you long ago, but this is the first time we've been together in so long."

Onlookers were talking and whispering amongst themselves. "Crazy vets."

Dwight looked Dobbs up and down. Dobbs had really straightened up since the last time Dwight had seen him. And he was back in uniform. He had rejoined the National Guard and was a Major. The last time Dwight saw Dobbs he looked like shit. He had turned into a drunk and drug addict and had tried to kill himself a couple of times. His wife divorced him and he was sleeping in abandoned cars. As a matter of fact, that was the same scenario for many of the 451 soldiers when they returned from Iraq. For some reason, they could not adjust to civilian life after all they'd been through. The 451 had the highest suicide rate of any battalion coming back from the Middle East. It was a real embarrassment for the National Guard and Colonel Price. After all the success they had in Iraq, then to come back and have the soldiers fall apart. What was going on? It was like a disease sweeping through the battalion.

"What changed for you?" Dwight asked Dobbs. "What helped you straighten up? You look great."

"It was a counselor I had in the VA. She really knew her stuff. She had never been in the military, but for some reason, she could identify. She told me to wave goodbye to those guys — to think of them as being on an inflatable raft, floating down the river, drinking beer, fishing, and having a good time. Wave goodbye to them, she told me. I did and things started straightening out for me."

"Well, I be go-to-hell," said Dwight. "You waved goodbye to them? So did I. We had the same counselor."

Later that day, a few of them, including Dwight, drove by the painted rock memorial in Grover, Iowa. It had Eddie Beams' picture painted on it, along with others. Dwight started to salute the image, caught himself, and instead, waved goodbye.

The following day, he had a goose hunting trip planned with one of his old 451 buddies, Miles Grogan. Miles spent the majority of his time hunting and fishing and just being outdoors. He had a lawn mowing business, and when he wasn't mowing, he was outdoors doing something. Most of the returning veterans were avid outdoorsmen.

Miles had a real good hunting dog, a Chesapeake Bay Retriever, that was a one-man dog. Miles loved that dog and took him everywhere. Wherever Miles was, the Chesapeake Bay Retriever named Hell, because he was "one hell-of-a-dog," was with him.

Being a retriever, Hell was a great duck-and-goose dog. He would charge into the water like a bull when the guns went off, and if Miles missed, Hell would come back and stare at him with a disgusted look. One time, Miles saw Hell retrieve two geese at one time in choppy water—he had them both by the neck—and laid the geese at Miles' feet.

On this day, Miles and Dwight had to walk a half mile through swampy ground to get to Miles' goose blind. It was a beautiful day and Dwight was enjoying walking. His hips and knees usually hurt, but for some reason, they were pain free. "Musta been that good cry I had yesterday," he said out loud.

"Huh?" Miles asked.

"Good creek. This here's a good creek feeding into the Upper Iowa."

"Oh, yeah. Sure."

A Gold Finch, Iowa's State Bird, landed on a weed in front of them, and displayed its golden color. "It's a little late in the season for finches, ain't it?" Miles asked.

"Maybe it's here just for us," mused Dwight. "A little piece of sunshine to brighten our day."

"Could be," Miles said. "Say, that's quite a gal in Brandy you have there. How'd you happen to snare that, you lucky son-of-a-buck?"

"To tell you the truth, I think God put her in my life. She was waiting for me on the jail house steps when I got released for that OWI."

"No shit? She looks like a keeper, awright. Better hang on to her."

"I intend to. We got one in the oven, you know."

"Yeah, I heard. Congratulations, Daddy."

"Thanks."

"By the way," Miles went on. "Do you ever get tired of them VA counselors asking you if you have PTSD?"

"Oh, yeah, sure. I guess," said Dwight. "I have it, so what the fuck? I just about hit the ground yesterday when that 21-gun salute went off."

"Yeah, me too. But I'm afraid they'll take away my Second Amendment rights if I admit I have PTSD."

(Miles carried a sidearm with him everywhere he went, as did most of the vets.)

"As a matter of fact," Miles went on, "I might get PTSD just by them asking me if I have PTSD. The ones who have problems, I think they were fucked-up before they went in."

"I dunno," Dwight sighed. "War is hell. It can screw with your brain. Miles, I pity anyone who tries to take away your guns."

"Yeah, me too."

Hell was bouncing in and out around them, trying to catch grasshoppers in his mouth. He would catch one, chew on it, and then spit it out, like it tasted bad, shaking his head, a scowl on his face. Dwight and Miles got a charge out of watching the antics of the magnificent retriever.

There was a little water in a ditch that was lined with switch grass. A rooster pheasant got up right in front of Hell, erping as it lifted in the air, and pooping. Hell instinctively jumped up and grabbed it. The rooster clawed at Hell's face and squawked. Hell started to bring the live bird to Miles, but the rooster was fighting so hard that Hell was having a hard time holding it. The pheasant's spurs were tearing at Hell's face and chest. Hell stopped and returned to the ditch, where he stuck the rooster under water. Hell waited a few seconds, brought the pheasant up, and it started scratching again. Hell stuck it under water a second time and held it a little longer.

Miles and Dwight were watching the dog and pheasant, their mouths open, shocked at what they were seeing.

When Hell brought it back up, there was still a little life left in the pheasant. Hell jammed the bird back under water and held it for a long time. When Hell brought it up the third time, there was no life left in the bird.

Hell brought the bird to Miles and laid it at his feet.

"Did you see that?" Miles screeched. "That dog knows how to drown a bird!"

"I saw it," Dwight said, amazed.

"That's instinct! You can't teach that."

Miles gave the pheasant to Hell to eat.

Miles and Dwight had a great day calling in geese to their decoys, shooting them, and watching Hell retrieve. Hell would get out of the water, a goose in his teeth, and then shower them with water as he shook off.

Dwight had a 12-gauge pump with bottom ejection, so the empty casings wouldn't hit his bird-blind partner. Miles had an over-under. Every once-in-a-while they traded guns. Both liked the other's gun better.

"Trade ya," said Dwight.

"Sure, I'll trade," said Miles. "But I'll need some boot."

"I'll boot you in the ass, awright," chuckled Dwight.

"I hate this aluminum bird shot they make us use now," said Miles, "instead of lead. It has no killing power. The other day I shot a mallard on the water. There was a perfect ring of shot around the bird. But it got up and flew away. I couldn't believe it."

"Yeah, but lead is so poisonous in the environment," said Dwight. "Pretty soon we'd've had no ducks. Trumpeter Swans are making a major comeback, also, since the removal of lead and certain pesticides."

"No ducks, sucks, I know. But I still like lead better."

Miles was so hard headed. God bless him, Dwight thought.

Dwight kept thinking about Hell holding the pheasant under water until it was dead. The dog did it naturally. Did humans kill naturally, too? From his experience in Iraq, Dwight thought, yes. Big brain or not, humans were really just animals, barely walking upright. Put enough pressure on them, and the right conditions, and they will kill because they want to.

That night in bed, Brandy took his hand and put it on her

swollen belly. The flutter he felt was like a dragon fly buzzing inside her tummy, not the sharp kick he was expecting.

Dwight dreamed about Black and Blankenship floating down the river, drinking beer, the sun shining on them. Herman Stein and John Washington appeared with them, also, and Eddie Beams.

They waved. Dwight waved back.